LIZ LOVELOCK

MY GUY #2

Cover Design by Ben Ellis from Be Designs
Photographer: Reggie Deanching from The Stable & Models of RplusMphoto
Models: Cody Smith and Tionna Petramalo
Edited by Lauren Clarke from Creating Ink and Swish Design & Editing
Proofread by Jen Lockwood Editing
Formatted by Tami at Integrity Formatting

www.lizlovelockauthor.com

MY
AUSSIE
Guy
MY GUY #2

CHAPTER
One

Elsie

My goodness, could they be any louder?

Lifting my head from the textbook I'd been studying, I check around for where the rowdy group are located. The library is meant to be quiet—a place where students can source their reference materials, reflect and read in silence. My gaze finally lands on a table where some of the basketball team—Jimmy, Dane, and one other unfamiliar person—are sitting. I'm guessing the new face is the exchange student from Australia we have all heard so much about. I can hear his accent quite clearly from my table across the room.

The noise is disrespectful to the library and everyone wanting to work quietly in here. I shake my head and turn back to Clifton. "Sorry, what were you saying?" I was sure I'd heard him asking me out. Again.

He clears his throat. "Did you want to go out sometime?"

I cringe.

Every week it's the same—he asks me on a date.

Every week it's the same answer—no.

"I'm sorry, Clifton. I have so much work to catch up on, and I'm booked up for tutoring. I don't really have the time." I meet his gaze and watch as his head drops. Guilt pours over me like hot liquid.

"That's okay. Perhaps when you have a little free time." Clifton shuffles his chair closer. Another one of his tactics. I nod, knowing full well that the date he desperately wants won't happen.

Clifton is a nice guy; he's just not my kind of guy.

Loud laughter fills the room again. I furrow my brow. I can't believe these boys.

"Excuse me a moment," I say to Clifton with a sigh. I'm thankful for this escape from him. At least it puts space between us.

I rise from my chair and stalk toward the noise. Their heads turn my way, and a sudden silence falls over their table.

I stop, standing over them with one hand on my hip. "Do you guys not understand that a library is for study and *silence?* You"—I cast my hand over the table, gesturing to them—"are all obviously not doing either."

Dane takes his cap from the table and puts it on his head. "Sorry, Elsie. We got a little carried away." Always the gentleman, that one. He's quick to fix the uncomfortable situations.

"More like a lot carried away. You're really loud, and how is anyone supposed to get any work done with you lot in here?" My eyes land on the new guy. He has dark hair and a perfectly chiseled jaw line with plump red lips. He's delicious.

My focus is trained on the new guy when Dane speaks. "Elsie, have you met Aiden? He's here for this semester."

So that's his name. I shake my head.

Aiden stands and extends his hand. "Nice to meet ya."

Oh, that sexy accent would make any girl swoon.

I take his hand. It's warm, slightly calloused, and he holds mine for longer than necessary. After a short moment, I withdraw it but there's still tingles which Aiden's touch left. Clearing my throat, I say, "Yep, you too. Now, can you all please shut up or leave? Some of us are trying to get work done." I gesture to Clifton across the room. I catch the hooded stare and disgusted look on Clifton's face. *Great, now I've done something to annoy him.*

"*Sure,* you're studying." Jimmy rolls his eyes then focuses behind me. "If looks could kill, I'm sure we'd all be dead right now. Guess your little friend over there doesn't like you talking to us." He lifts his hand and waves to Clifton with a cheesy grin splashed across his face. *Such a stirrer.*

My dagger-like glare falls on him. "What do you know, Jimmy? You're just a moody prick who enjoys annoying people for the hell of it."

Jimmy tips his head. *Smart ass.* "You're welcome." He laughs.

"We're going now. Just have to find the sign-up for tutoring," Dane says, standing from his chair.

"Front desk can show you what to do." I point them in the direction.

"Thanks for ya help." Aiden places his hand on my lower back as he passes behind me. The simple touch electrifies me. I spin toward him and watch him walk away with the guys until they stop at the front desk. His head turns back for a brief moment then faces the front again.

"Wow," I breathe. I cannot wait to tell my best friend, Addison, about him. It's possible she's already met him, considering she's in a relationship with the basketball captain, Parker.

I make my way back to Clifton. How am I supposed to concentrate now after meeting Aiden? The thought of him makes my heart stutter.

After I finish my tutoring classes for the evening, I head over to the basketball court. When I step through the door, my gaze falls on Addison across the court. I race toward her and Parker who stand on the far side of the stadium. "Oh my goodness, Addy, have you met the exchange student?"

I catch her flinch, and her hands go to her ears. All right. Settle down, Elsie, you're over-reacting.

"Oh, yes, Aiden?" she says.

"Why didn't you tell me he was drop-dead delicious? I had a run-in with him, Dane, and Jimmy at the library earlier today. They were being so disruptive." I huff, arms folded over my chest.

Parker nudges me. "Boys will be boys, Els. And look out, Aiden might have a crocodile as a pet." He laughs as he walks away shaking his head.

It takes me a moment to collect my thoughts. I catch Addison smiling like a goof as she watches Parker walk across the basketball court.

I playfully shove her shoulder. "Seriously, girl, you have it bad."

Her attention shifts back to me, and her smile is seriously

blinding. "So, this exchange student. What's he like? I haven't had much to do with him." We follow Parker across to where Dane, Jimmy, and Devon are standing.

"Yeah, I don't know. I only met him briefly; seems nice enough."

"I think Parker said he was going to come tonight. Are you going to hang around and watch the game?"

My feet grind to a halt. "Wait. What? Aiden is coming here tonight?"

She nods and keeps walking. It takes a moment for my brain to catch up with what Addison just said.

I race after her. "So, are you planning to stay?" she asks.

Shirtless, sweat-covered guys? Or lonely in my dorm doing homework? This one is a no-brainer. "Yeah, for sure. I've got no plans tonight. Are you playing?" She's such a sporty girl and not afraid to give things a go. I envy that part of her.

Addison shrugs. "I was going to, but I'm happy to watch as well."

"Yeah, I bet you are," I say sarcastically.

She turns and gives me a knowing glance. She's all about Parker these days. "Oh, shut it, Elsie. One day you'll find a guy and fall head over heels in love. Then, you'll be the one keen to do whatever your lover is doing. Come on. Let's go sit." She hooks her arm with mine, and we make our way to the bleachers and take a seat.

"Oi, what are you doing? You playing or what?" Parker shouts, waving his hand at Addison to try and get her on the court.

"There's no need. You have more than enough." She points to all the boys bouncing the ball and taking shots.

"Yeah, four is a good number," I agree.

"Oh, come on," Parker begs with a huge grin on his face. Addison shakes her head.

Gee, they're cute. *Snap out of it, Elsie. Your turn is coming.*

"All right, boys, two on two then," Parker says as the door swings open, and I about fall off my chair.

Aiden…

I spy, with my little eye, a shirtless Aiden.

Leaning over to Addison, I say, "Wow. I'd like to have a lick of that man candy."

She gives me a sidelong glance then busts out laughing, drawing the attention of Mr. Mancandy himself. I slap her. "Shut up. Don't draw attention to us."

I watch as Parker, Dane, and Jimmy casually walk up to Aiden while I bounce in my seat. "Oh my goodness, Addison." Excitement rips through me, and I want to throw myself down on the court and say, *"Take me, I'm all yours."*

"Keep your tongue in your mouth, woman," Addison says. I can see her trying to inspect him as he stands there talking to the guys.

Parker turns toward us. "Looks like you're up, Little Mouse. We have another player tonight. He's also on the basketball team."

Addison stands, and I follow. My chest vibrates.

"What if I don't want to play now?" Addison says with a hint of humor.

Before I can stop myself, I say, "I'll play."

All eyes turn on me. Parker cocks an eyebrow, a humorous smirk on his face. Addison's look mirrors his.

What the heck did I just say?

I look between all the shocked faces. A weight rests in my stomach.

Why didn't Parker mention that Aiden was on the team when I brought up the Aussie guy before?

Addison leans over and whispers, "Do you even know how to play?"

I take her arm and pull her across the hall, out of earshot of the guys. "What did I just say? I couldn't play if my life depended on it. I'm not a sports girl like you."

She laughs, shaking her head. "Just say you'll play another time and that you have an assignment to complete." Addison starts to walk away then pauses, looking back over her shoulder at all the guys who are now staring at us. "What has gotten into you? Or should I say, who?" She waggles her eyebrows.

I take a few deep breaths. "Okay, I can do this. Seeing Aiden has me all frazzled, and I hardly know the guy." The bouncing ball startles me as it echoes around the enclosure, and I look toward it. My nerves are jittery, causing me to jump at stupid sounds. Mr. Mancandy is taking shots with the guys. I watch his muscles flex with each move he makes.

"Wipe that drool you have coming from the corner of your mouth," Addison teases.

"I've got to go." She nods, and I take off, heading straight for the exit.

"Leaving so soon, Elsie?" Jimmy shouts.

I could kill him for trying to embarrass me.

I stop and turn toward him. "Yeah, I actually have an assignment that I have to finish. Sorry to disappoint. I'll kick your butt next time." I swear I hear him chuckling as I pull my shoulders back and strut to the door.

As I'm about to walk out, I look over my shoulder. Mr. Mancandy is watching me. He smiles and waves. I turn and attempt to leave, but instead, my forehead collects the doorframe, and I recoil.

"Ow, crap," I curse, putting my hand to my forehead. I race through the door and away from that stupid court. Gosh, I'm such a klutz. My legs carry me as fast as they will take me while my head has a small throb. *Can I crawl away and die now?*

"Hey, are you okay?"

I stop and slowly turn. My breath is coming fast. That voice. *It's him.* He saw the whole damn thing.

"Yes, I'm all good. Thanks for asking." *Act cool, Elsie. Don't embarrass yourself further.* I brush my hand over my already tidy hair and try to feign a chilled persona.

"Elsie, is it?"

I swallow and nod.

"Maybe next time you can join the game. I could give you a few pointers." He steps closer. The air in my lungs evaporates. My eyes fall on his pink lips. I want to lean up and press mine to his.

His voice snaps me out of my trance. "Anyway, I guess I'll see you around. Just wanted to check you were okay. I saw you hit your head." He points to the same place I whacked the doorframe on his own head. He leans right into me. My chest constricts. I close my eyes to breathe in his closeness. Then, he steps back and turns to leave, and I'm left out of breath.

"I guess I'll see you around, too," I whisper as I watch his bare muscular back strut back the way he came.

CHAPTER
Two

Aiden

"You good to go, man?" Parker asks as I walk back through the door to the basketball court. Images of the beautiful brunette imprint on my mind.

Nodding my head, I answer, "Yep, I'm good." Parker tosses me the ball. I dribble it up to the three-point mark and take a shot. When the ball sinks through the hoop, I recall when I brought up the idea to study abroad with my parents.

"I'm not sure that's a good idea," Mum said hesitantly. I'd wrangled my Aunt Wendy to take my side, *and* she suggested the trip.

"Give the boy a chance," Aunt Wendy's boisterous voice gave her opinion. "You've kept him under lock and key since he was little. It's time to loosen the reins." It's true. My family is wealthy, and I've attended the best schools, played in excellent sports teams, and never gone without. I think my aunt was trying to *not* let me turn into a lazy sod and mooch off my parents for the rest of my life. I am, however, more than thankful to be away from family and enjoying life right now, though.

"Why did you run after Elsie?" Parker's girl stands in front of me, her hand on her hip and a quizzical eyebrow raised. *What is her name again?* I wrack my brain, trying to remember. Parker pointed her and her friend out to me when I arrived, but I guess I was too distracted by Elsie to take notice of his woman.

"Uh… I was checkin' on her. She hit her head on the doorframe, so I was making sure she was all good." I shrug, wishing I had raced after the ball before Parker's girl bailed me up. What's the big deal? She's standing there with her hand on her hip still, her eyebrows arched and a smile on her lips. I'm not sure what the smile is all about. A part of me thinks she's analyzing me, sizing me up. Good luck to her. She's not going to get much information out of me.

"Addison, leave him alone."

Addison. That's right. That's her name.

She holds her hands out. "What? I'm simply saying hello." Her voice is high-pitched and all innocent. I get the feeling she uses this tone often. Does she not like me? Or did she not like me talking to Elsie?

This whole situation is becoming a little too uncomfortable for my liking.

Thank goodness Parker says, "Aiden, you're with Devon and Addison."

Is he serious?

My face must show my shock when Addison says,

"Don't worry. You might be surprised at my skills. Just don't be a ball hog." She grins—this time genuinely—then she walks away. *What is with this chick?* I must have done the wrong thing by checking on her friend.

I would have been happy having Elsie play, but I'm guessing she doesn't actually know anything about basketball.

"All righty, boys and girl, let's play," I announce, clapping my hands. "Three on three. What are we playing to?"

Parker answers, "First to twenty-five and half-court." He tosses the ball to me only to be intercepted by Addison. This girl has some quick moves. I'll give her that.

An hour later, I'm walking out of the basketball court door a loser—but only by one point.

"Didn't I tell you you'd be surprised?" Addison steps up beside me, Parker holding her hand.

I sure was. This chick and her brother couldn't hold their own. I was proven wrong.

"You were good. But we would have won if you'd got that last shot," I joke.

"Oh damn, snap!" Parker laughs, reaching around in front of Addison to high five me.

"Come on. It's all this guy's fault." She elbows him in the ribs.

"Now that's true."

When Addison was about to take the shot, he stepped up behind her—his distraction tactic. It totally worked, and she missed the shot.

We walk across campus, heading back to the house. Thankfully, there was space for me to move in when I arrived. Parker and the boys are pretty awesome. It's going to be hard for me to go back to Australia when my time here is up.

"Addison!" a familiar voice shouts.

All of us turn.

It's Elsie. Damn, she's so good-looking. Her long hair flows behind her as she runs to catch up to us. She has curves in all the right places.

"What happened to your assignment?" Parker teases.

I watch Addison glare at him while he continues to smirk.

"I finished it. What's it to you, anyway? I need to borrow Addison for a moment."

"Come back to the house. We'll get some food. You can talk to her there," Parker responds casually.

"What? Do you speak for her now?" she bites back.

Damn, she has serious sass. I like it.

Addison quickly jumps in. "No, he doesn't. I'm staying there tonight. Just come." She raises her eyebrows at Parker and releases his hand then moves and hooks her arm through Elsie's.

This exchange is weird. Have I somehow been placed with the most awkward group of people?

"I'm going to drop Devon home, and I'll meet you back at home," Dane says as he and Devon head toward his car which is parked on the side of the road.

I like the way they all look out for Devon—it's awesome.

I watch Elsie walking with Addison and Parker in front of me. This girl could be trouble. I can guess they're talking about me when both girls turn around and realize they've been busted. I smirk. This could be fun.

The girls quickly disappear when we get back to the house. Jimmy, Parker, and I are chatting about tonight's game when Elsie and Addison appear again. Elsie's looking rather flushed.

"Have any of you ordered the pizza?" Addison asks.

All three of us look between each other, and she's met with crickets. None of us have, and by the huff she releases, she knows it.

"Come on, guys, it's not up to the woman to deal with food. I'm not your slave. What did you do before I arrived?" She digs a phone out of her bag and steps away from the room to make a call.

Here's my chance to talk to her again. "Hey, Elsie, take a seat?"

She turns toward me as I pat the seat beside me with her eyebrows raised. "Yeah, okay, thanks." She hesitates a little but then makes her way to the seat beside me.

"I saw your name on the tutoring list when I signed up."

I watch as she processes the words, then slowly, she nods.

"Yeah. Ah… why mention that? Did you sign up under me?" Elsie shifts in her seat. Her fruity perfume floats around me.

"Wouldn't you like to know?" I tease, leaning back, studying her.

Elsie's eyes widen. She opens her mouth to respond, but we're interrupted when Addison comes back into the room.

"Pizzas are ordered," she says as she heads to the fridge and pulls out a soda.

"Did you get supreme?" Jimmy asks while he stares down at his phone.

Parker throws a cushion across at him. "Dude, she's not your slave. She's mine." He winks.

Jimmy shrugs, tossing it back at him. "She was ordering for everyone, wasn't she?"

"Calm ya tits, boys," Elsie says unexpectedly.

"Thank you, Elsie," Addison says as she walks to us and stands in front of Elsie. "Now, move over." For a split second, Elsie doesn't shift until Addison nudges her leg. A two-seater couch now squeezing three people on it. Elsie moves closer, and our arms rub against each other's. She becomes stock-still, and I swear I hear her breath hitch.

CHAPTER
Three

Elsie

What kind of game is Addison playing at? When we got here, she filled me in on tonight's game. She also told me she'd been sussing out Aiden. She reported all good things, and now she's trying to literally push us together.

Begrudgingly, I slide over closer to Aiden so Addison can sit on the couch. She's a sly one, this one. I know full well she'd usually sit on Parker's lap.

"What were you guys talking about before I came back in?" she asks.

"Aiden was asking Elsie about tutoring," Parker pipes up.

Could they be any more obvious? Since I saw Aiden at the court, I've been a mess. Flustered and all over the place.

I hardly know this guy, yet he's here, causing my brain to turn to mush and my heart to flip at every opportunity.

"Oh, you were, were you? Are you going to help him?" she asks me, glancing between us. I aim my glare at her, trying to tell her to stop with this—whatever it is she's trying to do. It's uncomfortable. I've known this guy all of five minutes, and here she is, trying to shove us together.

Thankfully, Aiden jumps in. "I already signed up today after meeting Elsie. She was one pissed-off chick." He laughs, tapping my arm.

My head turns toward him. "You guys were being loud and rude. Did you really expect anything different? Seriously, it's a library, for goodness' sake." I finally get a good look at Aiden. His warm, deep-brown eyes watch me. My heart leaps, and I find myself holding my breath for a moment. No guy has ever made me go gaga like Aiden does. Perhaps it's the Australian thing.

"So, Aiden, you keen for the game on the weekend? I think the coach is hoping you're as quick as your comebacks have been," Parker says. Jimmy laughs.

"Well, ya know, you losers can't be as good as me." Aiden grins.

Oh, hell, his smile is a chick magnet. I'm totally done for. I have zero chance with this guy.

"Please, I could run rings around you." Jimmy finally puts his phone down and looks over at Aiden.

"Seriously, boys, it's like a kindergarten in here." I laugh. "Is that all you guys do? Argue over who is better? You're on the same team, for goodness' sake." I stand and walk to the kitchen to retrieve a soda from the fridge. I shut the door and turn. My focus is on opening the bottle, and I almost collide with someone. "Oh, sorry."

I look up. It's Aiden, and we're inches apart. His hand

reaches out and touches my arm. *Is he trying to get close to me?*

"Excuse me," he says, his voice a whisper. Even two small words make my world shift.

"Oh, sorry." I step aside, out of his way. My face is flaming. Here I was thinking he wanted to get close to me. As usual, I am very wrong. My hands begin to shake for some unknown reason. *Why does he have this effect on me?* I hardly know the guy, and even if I did, I probably shouldn't get involved with him because he's only here on exchange and will be leaving in a few months.

All right, Elsie, snap out of whatever fantasy you have brewing in your crazy mind about Aiden and just be yourself.

Don't get attached. I repeat. *Do not get attached.*

A knock at the door brings Jimmy to his feet. "I've got it." Food makes that guy jump to attention.

"Anyone would think he's starving." Aiden laughs behind me.

I jump, not realizing he's that close, and step forward. "Ha, yeah, he is all about the food these days… and being a pain in the ass."

"Yeah, I'm slowly figuring that out," he says as he brushes past me, his chest sliding over my arm. Is he doing this on purpose? I'm sure there's plenty of room for him to go around me.

Stop analyzing everything, Elsie.

We eat in silence, and I swear I can feel eyes on me, but whenever I glance between them, no one appears to be paying any attention to me. I can feel it, though—a tingling up my back.

When we're all finished, I stand. "Well, I'm going to get going. Got a big day tomorrow with classes."

Addison jumps up from Parker's lap. *When did she move there?* Totally missed it.

She walks me to the door. "You are so quiet tonight," she whispers.

"I feel weird. It's so not me to be this silent."

"I know. You're freaking me out with this weirdness." She smiles.

"I'll move past it. It's just the newness about him that has me very intrigued. Plus, he's Australian. Who wouldn't fall for that? I'm sure every girl will be tripping over their panties to meet him."

We laugh. Addison hugs me.

As we part, Aiden steps out from the living room. "Let me walk you home."

Is he serious? "Ah… no, it's okay. It's only across the road." I wave my hand around, brushing off his offer. Secretly, I want him to walk me home more than anything.

"No, I'd rather you got home safely." Aiden sidesteps around me and opens the door. I give Addison a hug and call out bye to the other guys.

"Message me," Addison says as I move out the door with Aiden following closely behind.

"Will do. See you later." Stepping into the cool night air refreshes my frazzled brain.

"You good? You have everything?"

My hand drops to my phone in my pocket and my bag hanging off my shoulder, so I nod. "Yep, all good. You really don't have to walk me home… it's literally across the road," I say, clasping my hands together in an attempt to stop them shaking. He makes me nervous.

"Trust me. It's all good."

"All right. So long as you're sure." I must sound like a fool, repeating myself.

Aiden laughs. "Yes, I'm sure. Let's go."

A rather awkward silence falls between us. The street is quiet tonight as we come across no cars at all.

Aiden clears his throat. I look up at him. "So, do you actually play basketball?"

A heated flush warms my cheeks. Damn him. "I… ah… no, I don't, and I don't even know why I offered. I feel foolish. Hence the reason I smacked my head on the door as well. I was all over the place tonight." I laugh nervously. My stomach squeezes with dread.

"Why?"

Dude, what's with the twenty questions? And I can't even avoid them.

"Just because." I really don't want to have to explain that my reason was meeting him. That's downright embarrassing. I quickly jump in before he can bring up any more of my awkward moments tonight. "So, how long are you in America for?"

He shrugs. "I think a year. I'm not set on a date yet."

"Cool. Do you have a girlfriend back home?" I want to slap myself across the head. *Why did I ask that stupid question?*

Aiden is silent as we walk across the road and back onto campus grounds.

I sense he doesn't want to talk about it. "If you don't want to tell me, that's fine. I shouldn't have asked. Occasionally, I don't have a filter, and words just spill from my mouth."

Aiden shoves his hand into his pockets. "No, it's okay. I, ah… I have a girlfriend."

Double embarrassment. Here I am, being all nervous and hoping he likes me, and he has a girlfriend. Well, that sucks. All of a sudden, the excitement I had deflates like a balloon.

I rub my neck. "That's cool. I bet you miss her."

"Yep. I do." I look up at him, and his eyes are averted from mine, unlike earlier when he sought the connection. "So, do you think you could help me with tutoring?"

Thankful for the change of subject, I say, "Yeah, sure, but you'll have to go to the library to fill out a form. Sorry. It's so I can keep track of who I'm working with. It's so I don't overdo things and not get my own work done."

"Yeah, all good. I did that today."

We reach the café, and my dorm is only one more block. "You don't have to walk me the whole way... my dorm is in the next building. Thanks for walking me back, though."

"It's fine. I couldn't let you walk on your own. I look forward to getting to know you, Elsie."

"You, too, Aiden. You never know... when all this apparent awkwardness disappears between us, and our friends stop trying to push us together, we could actually have a good friendship..." I pause. My hand lifts up, and I slap myself on the forehead. "I'm so sorry. Word vomit."

Aiden laughs harder than he has tonight. It's a relief, actually. I was beginning to think he thought of me as a crazy person.

"You're a crack-up, Elsie. I'll see you tomorrow." He pats me on the back and turns.

"See you then." I walk away with a smile on my face, but deep down, I feel a little hurt.

He has a girlfriend.

I shouldn't be feeling like this.

Pull yourself together, Elsie. We can be friends, at least.

CHAPTER
Four

Elsie

"Oh, he's here!" My fingers curl around Willow's arm, latching tightly, digging into her soft skin. She flinches and follows my line of sight. *Aiden.* I hadn't seen him around since he walked me home on Monday night. I scan the room again for Addison and Parker, momentarily removing my stare from him. They haven't arrived yet. Where could they be?

It's another weekend party. I love a good party, especially when there is a new guy in town whom I'm trying to impress and prove I'm not a crazy girl. So far, I've failed miserably. And now that I know he has a girlfriend, there's no pressure on me to even try.

The basketball team crushed their opponents again tonight. My eyes were all for Aiden and watching how he played since it was his first game for the season. Parker scored the winning shot, and boy was it a hair-raising moment. I thought it was going to bounce out of the ring and not sink through the net. The crowd went crazy, people standing on their seats. The cheering was the loudest I'd ever heard in the stadium when the ball sank through the hoop.

Willow, Jane, and I have crashed the basketball team's house for their party. Technically, it's not really crashing if our friend is dating the basketball captain.

A drink is thrust into my hand. Turning to my left, I see Jane handing it to me.

"Thanks." I smile. We stand in the corner of the room and peruse the fellow partygoers. My eyes always find their way back to Aiden. I must seem pathetic. I'm swooning after a guy I don't know and can't even have. He has about five girls hanging off him now. *Good luck, girls*. But I want him to make eye contact with me.

Stacey struts up to him. She doesn't seem to care. He's already talking with Laura from English, and she pretty much throws her boobs in his face. *Honestly! What a ho*. It's pretty embarrassing to watch. I groan.

"Stop staring, Elsie. He has a girlfriend." Addison's playful words cut into my trance. I turn to look at her with raised eyebrows.

She's holding hands with Parker and is practically glowing. "You." I point a finger at Parker. "Why didn't you tell me he has a girlfriend?" This was the first time since Monday I've seen him.

Parker's mouth falls open. Still, he says nothing. He steps back and pretty much hides behind Addison.

"I made a damn fool of myself, and this one here didn't help." I stomp my foot and point to Addison. I swing my attention to her. "Are you sure you didn't know? I mean, you told me you didn't, but why didn't he say something to the guys?" I cross my arms over my chest, pursing my lips.

"What? No! If Parker or I knew, I would have told you. You know me better than that."

I throw my arms around her, giving her the tightest bear hug. She *would* have told me. I think my drinks are starting to take effect. My snappy, chatty drinking self is coming out to play.

"Elsie, he didn't tell us. You're the first person he's told. I haven't heard him on the phone to anyone other than his parents and sister. But I'm not saying he hasn't got one; he just doesn't mention her." Parker laughs. I cross my arms over my chest, not wanting to talk about it anymore. *If only that were true.*

I release my hold of Addison and assess what she's wearing—tight black jeans and a red fitted shirt. She looks hot. Her long brown locks always sit perfectly. "Looks like you're finally starting to want to dress up," I tease, letting her go.

She shoves me playfully. I step back. "Shut up. Not everyone can be a supermodel like you." Addison nods toward my body.

Tonight, I chose a simple black dress. It sits above my knees. I figured showing a little leg and subtle curves on display won't hurt anyone. It also makes me feel sexy and confident, although I'm not feeling either of those things in this moment. I want to be strutting up to the Aussie guy and hitting on him without a worry about what he'll think. But I'm not, because I'm not the type to come between a couple. I have a zillion butterflies wreaking havoc on my stomach every time I catch a glimpse of him. I can't keep my emotions in check. More alcohol is definitely needed, so I throw back another mouthful of my drink.

"Have you spoken to him again?" Addison asks.

"No way. I'd probably embarrass myself even more." I recall my head hitting the doorframe. Gosh, I must have looked stupid.

"He's actually a nice guy. I've had a few chats with him over the last couple of days," she says. *Of course, she would have.*

I grip her shoulder with my free hand. "I haven't seen his name on my list for tutoring, so perhaps I scared him off."

Addison's eyes light up, a hint of mischief in them. She leans into me and says, "Here's your chance to find out if he signed up."

I spin around as Aiden stops beside Parker.

"Hey, man. Wicked party," he greets Parker.

I freeze. My eyes go wide and connect with Addison's. She smiles. I want to run away and hide.

His accent—*swoon.*

My stomach flips upside down upon hearing it.

Oh. My. Goodness.

"Thanks. Thought we were going to lose, though." Parker and Aiden strike up a conversation about the events of tonight's game.

Slowly, I remove my hand from Addison's shoulder and down the rest of the drink. I need another. Liquid courage. As if someone has read my mind, two shots are put in my vision. Jane takes my empty cup, and Willow gives me the shots. I throw them back, and they settle in the pit of my stomach. Tequila. Damn, Willow and Jane know my weakness. This drink gets me chatting and crazy all the time. It loosens me up, which is just what I need tonight.

I turn and stand beside Addison. Willow and Jane are on her opposite side. None of us are speaking. Our attention is on the guys in front of us who are chatting like they've been friends forever.

It's as if there's a glow around Aiden. He appears carefree and confident. *Cocky and confident* may be better terms. His dark hair is smoothed back and sits neatly. The dark-blue jeans he's wearing are tight and show off his perfect ass, which is appealing to the eye. He's also wearing a white button-up shirt with the sleeves rolled up. Those tattooed arms make my stomach twist—in a good way. *Damn.* I'd love to know what it feels like to be wrapped in them.

Parker's words bring me to attention. "Aiden, this is Jane, Willow, and of course, you've already met Elsie." When Parker gestures to me, heat rises in my face. I wave hello, but I'm mute. *How damn stupid must I look?*

"Nice to meet you, lovely ladies." Aiden's focus stops on me.

I think I might pass out.

He shakes Willow's and Jane's hands.

I'm caught in some sort of trance.

Aiden's grin as he greets the girls stabs me in the chest. *Why does he bring me to my knees?*

When he gets to me, I'm a statue. A deer caught in the headlights. My focus is stuck on him. I know he's got his hand in front of me, but mine feels like lead. Come on, body, take his hand.

"Has this one become defective since I last saw her?" Aiden laughs as does everyone else. "Did the bump on the head cause short-term amnesia?" His hand drops, going back to his side.

Dead.

I am dead.

But his question snaps me out of my stupid trance. My hand goes to my hip, my chest pumping with sass. "Who are you calling defective, buddy?"

"And… she speaks." He waggles his eyebrows, raising his hands.

"Sorry, my attention must have been elsewhere," I say. "What's your name again?" I don't hide the sarcasm dripping from my words. I decide to go along with his game of not knowing who I am, considering I've already met him.

Aiden holds his hand out, and I slip mine into his firm grip. A tingle spreads from my fingertips right to my hammering heart.

"Aiden. Nice to meet you… Elsie, was it?" He tilts his head to the side. I catch the mischievous glint in his eyes.

"Don't play coy. You know my name." I roll my eyes. My confidence starts to return.

Aiden doesn't release my hand, and I don't make a move to let go of his. The air around us crackles.

He grins before letting go. Looking around the group, all eyes are on us.

"Just checking to see if you still knew your name," he teases.

Silence falls between us.

Addison speaks up, probably to attempt to cover the weirdness Aiden and I have created. "So, are you liking it here, Aiden?"

He turns his attention to Addison while I blow out a breath. "Yeah. I love the beach. Some awesome waves to ride out there." He pauses for a moment then says, "I've heard there's a spot people go where they can jump from a cliff into the ocean. They said it's not super high, but it's fun. I'm down for that kind of stuff."

I know the place he's talking about. Before I can stop myself, I say, "Yeah, Crow's Peak."

Now his heavy gaze is back on me.

"You know the place?"

"Yes," I reply slowly, wishing I didn't open my big mouth.

"Wanna show it to me sometime?"

"Yeah, sure. You let me know when. We'll see how much of a wimp you are," I tease. *Why the hell am I agreeing to this?* It's as if he's put a spell over me, and I can't back down from anything he suggests.

Wait. What just happened? I'm the wimp when it comes to that cliff. I've never been able to bring myself to take the leap, and I've just said yes to taking Aiden there. I suppose I didn't commit to actually jumping, though.

Aiden bursts out laughing. "I like you, firecracker. You're quick with your words." He steps up to me, his face inches from mine. "Bring. It. On. If I jump… you have to jump." His breath hits my lips, and it smells of a mixture of alcohol and mint.

I stand a little taller. The heat between us intensifies while I swallow the nervous twinge in my throat. "I'm ready whenever you are." I dig my hole a little deeper.

Aiden straightens up. His gaze holds mine. "Tomorrow, then?"

As much as I want to say no, I somehow find myself nodding.

"Perfect!" he announces.

Oh my God. My legs go weak, wanting to collapse beneath me.

An arm loops through mine. *Willow.*

"Sorry, you can't have her tomorrow. She's got to work at the café. All day."

Note to self: *thank Willow later.*

"All right, firecracker. Next Saturday. You, me, and Crow's Peak."

"You're on," I squeak, already wanting to rewind this conversation and eliminate myself from the equation.

Why didn't I just say no?

CHAPTER *Five*

Aiden

Why did I lie?

If I hadn't told that one white lie about a pretend girlfriend, I wouldn't feel as guilty as I do right now. I've pretty much set her up for a dare I'm sure she won't follow through with. Because of this lie, I've set myself up to look like a cheater if I even try to get close to her. *Aiden, you're a fool.*

Addison steps up to Elsie. "Are you sure about this?" she whispers.

Elsie shifts. Her gaze turns to Addison. "Never been surer."

I'm going to have to tell the truth. This girl is a

firecracker, one who draws my attention, and there seems to be this invisible rope wrapped around us, pulling us closer together. I told the white lie to protect not only myself but Elsie as well, because when I leave, it's going to break whoever it is I end up with.

"You can back out anytime you want," I say, really wishing she would. I hadn't even been game to sign up for her tutoring because she is who she is. I can already see she's showing interest in me. It's blindingly obvious, and considering the daily questions from Addison when I see her at the house, I can't help but be thinking about Elsie constantly.

Elsie shoves my shoulder. "No way, mate." She accentuates the *mate,* attempting an Australian accent. I laugh. "Only if you back out."

"No, you're on. I'm an extreme sports person. For you, I'll do something a little easier. Let me take you fishing, if you think you can handle it."

Elsie's face screws up, and I think I've got her on that one. "Sure, I'm down for it." *This girl doesn't give up.*

Addison looks at me with a small grin on her face. "Something you need to know is, no matter the dare, Elsie *has* to follow through. If she's given a challenge, no matter what it is, and no matter how much it frightens her, she *has to* do it. It could also be because it's you that is issuing the challenge. So, you might want to stop throwing dares at her like confetti, because she'll take you up on it any day." There's a firmness to her words, and I can tell they ring true. Great! So now I've set her up for two things in one night. This is going to be interesting.

How am I supposed to not show any interest in Elsie and risk her getting hurt, or me looking bad because of my lie?

Elsie stands there in her black dress, her hands on her hips. She's totally not the quiet girl I thought she was on

Monday night. She has sass, which is making quite the appearance tonight.

"Is that true?" I ask Elsie.

Her eyes don't move from mine as her lips pull up on one side, and she shrugs. "I can't help it. It's who I am."

"This could be fun. I'll be careful what I throw at you next," I tease. As I do, her eyes bulge. "Easy, I'm set with just these two for now." I rest my hand on her shoulder, and I sense her stiffen, so I remove it as quickly as I put it there. *Am I putting out the wrong signals?*

"Do I really have to go fishing? The smell is just nasty." She pretends to dry-retch.

"It's not that bad. I'm sure you'll survive. You know you can back out if you want."

"What? No way. I'm not letting you win," she snaps, shoving me in the chest. I step back, grinning.

Now I somehow have to try and not fall for her. I'm scared to get too close. When I came to America, I decided not to start a relationship with any girl. Reason being, I don't want to hurt anyone, but more importantly, I want to protect myself from the pain of leaving them behind.

So far, my plan is not going well.

CHAPTER Six

Elsie

What the hell have I done?

I'm great at putting on a brave face, but right now, everything inside of me is screaming. Cliff jumping and smelly fishing. The thought turns my stomach. Aiden stands there with a smug look on his face, his eyebrow cocked as if to dare me to pull out, but I won't give him that satisfaction.

"Well, I guess I'll see you next weekend. But for now, I need to hit the dance floor." Without giving him the chance, I turn and take Willow's arm and pull her along with me.

"Are you really going to do that?" she asks, a little unsure.

"Yep. I don't know why but I can't back out. I really wish I could, though. You know me and heights."

She gives me a knowing look.

"Anyway, let's get another drink and let me drown my fears." My heart races merely thinking about it. The thought of jumping from that cliff into the ocean makes me feel physically sick. My stomach tightens, and I really want to back out of this stupid dare. Now, though, I can't. It's not in me to show weakness.

We make our way to the kitchen, where the drinks are located, when a shoulder pushes against mine somewhat hard. "Ow… watch where you're going!" I turn, yelling at whoever it is.

Clifton's standing there with a smirk on his face. "Oh, I'm so sorry, Elsie." Clifton is on the football team. I tutor him for math. He's a nice enough guy. Tall, olive complexion and a pair of seriously blue-as-blue eyes. They were the first thing I noticed about him.

"Watch where you're going. I'm not someone you're out to tackle. You'd snap me in two." I laugh, and so does he.

"So, are you enjoying the party?" he asks, shoving his hands into his pockets and swaying back on his heels. I haven't paid much attention to him since he's just not my type, other than helping him with his work. I'm not like his football groupies. Nope, not going to happen. Although, come to think of it, I forgot to ask Aiden about his tutoring.

I managed a few new sign-ups this week but didn't see his name. I also had one sign-up for online help. With online, you don't really know who it is—they tend to use anonymous interface. They do that because they're embarrassed they need help, which is fine. Personally, I think it's great; at least you can still get some help.

"Yeah, I'm enjoying myself. Always do." I smile.

He grins back. "All right, well, I guess I'll see you on Wednesday for tutoring."

"Yep, you will. Don't be late this time."

Clifton's hand goes to his chest like my words have hurt him. "Who, me? I'm never late."

I roll my eyes. "Yeah, yeah, whatever you say, Cliff. A couple of weeks back, you didn't even show up."

"Yeah, sorry about that. Had practice."

Willow takes that moment to step away from me, leaving me with Clifton.

"Email me next time so I'm not wasting my time waiting on you."

Clifton nods, then he unexpectedly steps closer to me. *Dude, what are you doing?*

I take a small step back. "Ah, Cliff… can I help you with something?"

Cliff's hand rises and rakes through his blond hair. Those blue eyes hold my gaze—they appear slightly crazed. I'm not sure if I want to run or stand my ground, but I choose to stay. He leans into me, his mouth near my ear, his breath tickling my neck. "I was hoping you'd go out with me some time."

Stepping back, I put a good amount of distance between us. "Don't get me wrong, Cliff. I like you, but not like that." Please don't take it the wrong way.

Again, he moves closer to me, and alarm bells start sounding in my head. "Please, Elsie. I'd like one chance to go out on a date with you. Not tutoring… an actual date." His breath hits my nose—it's a mixture of pizza and vodka. *Eww, so not nice.*

Tightness pulls at my chest. The look on his face tells me he means what he's saying, but I've known him for a while now. He's very much a ladies' man. "Look, how about you come to me when we're both sober, and we can talk about it then?" I nod to myself, happy with my answer. I'm sure he won't remember this conversation tomorrow. I look to my left and catch Aiden watching the weird exchange.

A hard look rests on Aiden's face. *What's his problem?*

Then, Clifton is at my ear again.

I jump back this time. "Dude, I gave you an answer. Talk to me about it when you're not simply trying to get in my pants." I hold my hands out, stopping him from advancing.

Clifton waggles his eyebrows. "Oh, Elsie. Let's get out of here."

He's drunk. The smell of his breath is enough to turn off any girl here.

"That's not going to happen. I'll see you on Wednesday." Turning my back to him, I notice Aiden has moved closer to Clifton and me. It's as though he's about to pounce on Clifton.

I step toward him, taking his arm and pulling him away. "Don't even go there. I see what you're thinking of doing. He's just drunk. I tutor him." I don't even bother glancing back at Clifton. That boy's not worth the drama.

"He looked like he wasn't going to leave you alone. I was only going to step in if it was needed."

"Aw, look at you being my superhero. Sorry, Superman. I am no Lois Lane needing rescuing all the time, though." I laugh, playfully shoving his arm, which I realize I'm still holding onto. My chest constricts as I know I need to let go, but I really don't want to. My body ignites with sparks, leaving a tingling sensation swimming through all parts of me.

"No, you don't need saving. You're a little firecracker who will explode on anyone who gets in your way. Am I right?"

I tap his arm. "You get me. Well, you don't know me entirely yet, but I'm sure you will. We'll be great… friends." I push the word out of my throat, not wanting it to leave. We will be great friends, and then he'll go home to his girlfriend where everything will go back to normal. That's what's going to happen.

Finally, I let go of his arm.

Aiden and I arrive in the kitchen just as Willow steps into the doorway. "How could you leave me with him?" I scold her then snatch one of the drinks from her.

She glances between Aiden and me. "What are you talking about? It's just Clifton," she says, not really caring so much about why I'm so annoyed.

"He, like, full on came on to me and wanted me to go out with him. Then, big guy here was going to take him on to rescue me." I backhand Aiden in the chest. He crouches forward, obviously not ready for my hit. A puff of air pushes out of his mouth.

Willow's face drops. "I'm so sorry. I thought he was harmless." Her arms fly around me.

"It's all good; he backed off." I smile. "I guess we should get back to enjoying this party and the free booze," I say, hugging her back. I glance up at Aiden, and he smiles down at me. My stomach flips, and then I remind myself he's taken, and I step out of Willow's arms and down a shot she's poured.

Why, oh why, does he have to have a girlfriend?

CHAPTER
Seven

Elsie

I sit on the outskirts of the campus field, under a tree, while watching students running laps. Today is a beautiful day. The sun is hot and there's a light breeze floating around. I open my laptop. I have an email to respond to about tutoring.

I connect my phone's Bluetooth to the laptop for the internet. I should cut back on tutoring, but then it'd be like I was letting those students down. If it becomes too much, I'll pull right back, but right now I am doing okay, and the money is good.

While waiting for my computer to catch up, I recall last night, and the challenges Aiden has given me. I inwardly cringe thinking about them. Thankfully, Willow saved me by saying I had to work today. I'm not prepared for this.

After the Clifton episode, Aiden stayed pretty close. We chatted, and when I went off to dance, I would catch him watching me. Perhaps that's wishful thinking. It was nice, in a way. I wonder what his girlfriend is like. I bet she's super gorgeous—supermodel-like.

"You had to work, huh?"

My head flicks up, and my hand flies to my chest. "What the hell?"

Aiden is standing beside the tree trunk, looking down at me. My heart is pounding a million miles an hour. Well, it feels like it is. I knew I should have left campus grounds. He did tell me last night that he was going out today, so I thought I'd be safe here. Boy, was I wrong. I look at my watch—it's close to lunchtime. Time has slipped away from me.

Aiden moves and sits on the grass beside me. His knees are up, and his arms rest over them. "So, what happened to working?" he asks, cocking his head to the side, eyebrows raised. *Busted.* I could lie and say I only worked this morning.

"The truth is, I didn't actually work. Addison was saving me." I nervously look around and avoid his gaze. Trust me to be the one to get caught out in a fib.

"Ah, well, I kind of guessed it when I didn't see you at the café this morning."

I turn to him. "Are you checking up on me?"

Aiden's now the one avoiding eye contact. "Ya know, just wanted to see how ya pulled up after last night. You were kind of hanging off me by the end of it. Literally… hanging off me. I had to carry you back to your dorm."

"You did not. I would remember you taking me back home." My voice raises. I didn't think I was that bad. *Oh, goodness, how silly was I?* I don't recall anything bad happening. "I think you're lying, because I can remember everything that happened. Are you sure you weren't the drunk one and are making sure you didn't cheat on your girlfriend—"

I stop, pulling my lips tightly closed. I shouldn't continue saying 'with me' because that's asking for trouble. I quickly backtrack. "So sorry… honestly, that came out all wrong. At times, my filter doesn't work. That's not something to joke about."

Aiden looks away from me again. He's holding a small twig between his fingers, and as he moves it, he snaps it into smaller pieces. After a moment, he finally turns to me, and I notice there's no smile on his face.

"You didn't do or say anything wrong. I just… ah… miss my girlfriend." Gee, don't choke on the word, buddy.

"Oh, I'm sorry. What's her name?" I ask gently, cautious of his reaction.

Another small silence. "Ah… Emma."

"Nice. What does Emma think of you being over here?" I close my laptop, completely interested in what he's about to tell me about his girlfriend.

Aiden shifts around on the grass as if he's uncomfortable. "She wasn't too happy, but I had planned this trip for a while, so I was always going to do it whether I was in a relationship or not."

"That's fair enough. How long have you been together?"

His brown eyes turn to me. There's something there, but I'm not sure what. It's as though he wants to say more, but he keeps his mouth shut. That is, until he finally answers my question. "Only a short while." He shrugs. Before allowing me to say anything else, he blurts out, completely changing the subject, "Anyway, what are your plans for the rest of the day? You wanna go grab a bite for lunch, or can I hold you to one of your dares?" He waggles his eyebrows.

I cross my arms in front of me. "Yeah, I'm not doing any of those today. I have a raging headache, and I'm sure jumping from a cliff won't help that. And don't even get me started on the foul stench of fish." I pretend to gag. Aiden laughs. Not just any laugh, but a full-on belly laugh. I can't help but smile at him enjoying himself at my expense.

"Gee, you remind me of my little sister. The way you said that right then... it was her. Only when my sister says it, it's said with an Australian accent."

"You have a sister?"

"Yeah, Eden. She's fifteen."

"That's so cool."

"Do you have any brothers or sisters?"

"I do. An older brother who's off traveling the world right now. He finished college and decided he needed time away. Kinda like you, in a way." I backhand his arm. We fall into a comfortable conversation. At least, I'm slowly getting to the point of not carrying on like a fool around him. Even if there is a part of me that still wishes he didn't have a girlfriend.

Aiden nods. "Sounds like my kinda guy. I want to do more traveling when this semester is over. I seem to have picked up a travel bug in my teen years."

I lean back against the tree trunk and look up at the blue, cloudy sky. "I would love to travel. Take time for myself instead of study. Don't get me wrong, I want an education and all that, but there's a big part of me that wants to get out of this small town."

He stretches his legs out and leans back on his hands.

"You should come to Australia for a holiday. I can show you around."

"Pfft, yeah… I bet your girlfriend would love that." Sarcasm drips from my words.

"I'm sure she'd be fine."

"Doubt it. If I were your girlfriend, I wouldn't like another chick hanging off you. I'd make sure others knew you were mine." My hand goes to my mouth. "And there I go again, foot in the mouth. Sorry." I chew my bottom lip, waiting for him to say anything.

Aiden stands, and dread fills me. I'm sure he's walking away because I'm such a fool. Stupid, broken filter. He turns, looking down at me. "I'd be happy for you to be all protective…" He smiles. "If you were my girl, that is." Clearing his throat, he continues, "Get ya stuff together, and let's go get lunch."

Without hesitation, I shove everything in my bag. Aiden holds his hand out to me, and I take it. It slips perfectly into his and, for some reason, feels right. He pulls me off the ground with ease, only he doesn't release my hand as quickly as I thought he would, so I glance up at him. He opens his mouth then shuts it, his lips forming a thin line. He drops my hand, and I'm left confused.

What was that all about?

CHAPTER
Eight

Aiden

*D*amn, I'm digging myself into a hole I'm not sure how I'll get out of. Elsie is so upfront. I'm so scared I'm going to say something that will reveal my lie. The lie that is slowly killing me. I've done this for a reason, and I have to stick to it.

After we had lunch today, she had to leave to do homework, and I needed to get in contact with her as my tutor, only she shouldn't know it's me. Well, I hope she doesn't. Thankfully, she didn't ask me about signing up to her services today. I, for sure, thought she would have. I have to have this English essay handed in over the next couple of weeks, and I haven't done much work on it, just typed out what I thought was somewhere near right and that's it. Now, I've found out that to continue on the basketball team, my grades need to be up to scratch, or I'll be benched. That's not my idea of fun.

I'm sitting at the kitchen counter when Parker walks through the door. I turn and wait for Addison and, hopefully, Elsie to follow. When they don't, I can't help the disappointment that fills me.

"What are you up to, man?" I ask casually before facing my computer again.

"Not much. Got homework to do for next week. Hey, do you want to come to the movies tonight? Addison, Elsie, Paislee, myself, and the guys are all going."

My interest is piqued. Another chance to talk to Elsie.

"Sure. I'll finish this email."

Parker nods, opening the fridge. He takes a water bottle out, sculls it in one go, then he walks out of the kitchen, heading toward his room.

Now, what am I supposed to say in this email?

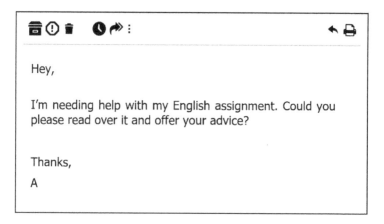

Hey,

I'm needing help with my English assignment. Could you please read over it and offer your advice?

Thanks,
A

I think that's simple enough, and I'm sure Elsie won't know it's me. I attach my document to the email and hit send. When I get up from the stool, my phone starts to ring. Looking down at it on the bench, my sister's caller ID is blinking through Facebook messenger.

"Hey, sis. What's goin' on?"

"Not much. Just wanted to check in and see how you were doing? Made lots of new friends?" Always nosey, my sister. She may only be fifteen, but she has the brains of the family. I'm the sports and all-outdoors-type stuff, and she's always got her nose in a book.

"You know me, I'm forever making new ones." I slide back onto the stool and shut my computer.

"What about *girlfriends?*" The way she says girlfriends really shows her age. I can't help but roll my eyes. She is always onto me about girls for some strange reason.

"What's it to ya?"

"Come on, Aiden. Tell me?" she whines.

I toss up about discussing my lie, but I'm sure she'll scold me. She's so much like Mum, even if she denies it.

My free hand taps the bench as I look over my shoulder to make sure no one is around. I lower my voice. "In case you must know, there are no girls… I've kind of created a white lie."

She groans. Yeah, I figured that would be her reaction, and I cringe upon hearing her. I don't need her disapproval. I already know I've done the wrong thing. The only problem is I don't know how to rectify it.

"What kind of lie?" I can hear the disgust in her words. Immediately, I know this is a bad idea and I shouldn't tell her. "Don't go changin' your mind now. You have to tell me what stupid thing you've done."

"I already know it's a stupid thing I've done. I don't need you grillin' me about it. I know you."

"You need all the grillin' you're going to get. Now, tell me so I can talk a little sense into that thick skull of yours," she demands.

I look over my shoulder again—no one's around. "I told people I have a girlfriend back home."

"You did *what?*" she yells into the phone so highly pitched that I pull it away from my ear with a wince.

"Yeah, I know." I sigh.

"How could you be so stupid? You fool. You're better than that. Why didn't you simply say you don't want to be in a relationship?"

I rub my free hand down my face. "I know. I made a mistake. I did it because I didn't want to hurt anyone when it came time for me to leave. The last thing I need is to leave behind a broken heart. I thought I was doing the right thing." My stomach tightens with dread. I already know that Eden is going to tell me to come clean before she says it.

"You need to be honest with the people in your circle over there, or you'll burn bridges. Is there anyone who's caught your eye?"

I can hear the wheels turning in my sister's little mind already. She doesn't miss anything.

Clearing my throat, I say, "There is one who has, but I told her I had a girlfriend. She seems cool with it. We're just friends." Although, the pull I feel toward her only seems to be getting stronger the more I spend time with her.

"What the hell, you stupid brother of mine," she yells once again.

"Eden, calm down. You're carrying on a bit silly."

"Blah, blah, blah… I'm carrying on. Have you looked in the mirror lately? You're the one telling lies. I understand your reasoning, but you're stupid. Stupid!" Her voice is still raised as she continues talking, but I don't hear because a throat clears, startling me, from behind. I flick around, and Parker's standing there with his brow furrowed as he stares right at me.

"Uh… Eden, I have to go."

"Don't do that to me now. We aren't finished. I need to tell you how stupid you are again."

"I get it. I'll talk to you later. Catch ya." I don't give her a chance to say goodbye. I hang up, my eyes not moving away from Parker's.

There's a moment of silence before he speaks. "So, the girlfriend is a lie?" There's no emotion in his words, and I instantly know I've betrayed his trust.

I nod. "It is. I didn't want to risk anyone getting hurt when I leave, so I thought it would be easier, but it's not."

Parker steps closer. "Why didn't you just tell the truth from the start? I'm sure everyone would have accepted that. Now you've done so much worse."

I flinch. His words sting, because he's right. I could have gone about this in a completely different way.

I groan. "I know. How can I fix it?" I ask, hoping he has a way to get me out of this.

"Easy. Tell the damn truth. There was no girlfriend to start with." He slaps me on the shoulder.

"All right. I'll figure it out."

"Good. Until you tell everyone, I'll say nothing. It's not my secret—or should I say lie—to tell. Just don't wait too long."

"Yeah, okay, thanks."

"Now, go get ready. We have to meet the others."

I leave the kitchen with my laptop tucked under my arm. Walking to my room, the thought of coming clean about my lie kills me.

One thing is for sure. Elsie, with all her sass, is sure to hate me.

We're all waiting around in the cinema after getting our tickets when I see who's here. It's like a couples group date. And here I am, a lone ranger, or the fifth wheel.

Parker stands there with his arm around Addison's waist. Dane is standing beside Parker's sister—I think her name is Paislee. I don't believe they're together, but if they're trying to hide something, they're not very good at it. I catch them whispering, but Parker seems completely oblivious to it all. *Gee, he's not on the ball.* I've been around them for the first time tonight, and I saw it within the first fifteen minutes.

"What happened to Jimmy?" I ask Parker. I thought he was coming tonight.

He turns his attention to me. "He wanted to go to the gym instead. Couldn't be bothered going to a movie. That's just him; he changes his mind all the time." Jimmy is a moody type of guy. Not very friendly either, but Parker seems to handle him well enough. I don't think he's warmed to me yet. Hasn't really given me the time of day.

I have bigger problems to worry about, though.

"Okay, cool," I reply to Parker when I'm shoved in the arm. Turning toward it, I see Elsie standing with a brilliant white, perfect smile. Immediately, my breath is kicked from my lungs.

"Hey there, friend," she says playfully as she shoves a handful of popcorn in her mouth. Damn, if only she knew what a tease she was being right now.

"Hey, how was the rest of your day?" I ask, shoving her back while I move slightly closer. She smells like berries with a dash of spice.

"I slept. After last night, I needed it. I was wrecked." She laughs, shuffling on her feet. Elsie's in these perfectly fitted jeans, which hug her body nicely, and a pink T-shirt. She's perfection. She's hardly wearing any makeup and has blush-pink lips. I bite on my bottom lip as I assess her. She's gorgeous.

How could I have let myself tell that lie?

Now, how do I go about telling Elsie the truth?

Not going to happen tonight.

"All right, guys. Let's go. I bet we're going to have to sit separate because it's a new movie," Dane says as he takes off toward the cinema with us all following. Elsie stays beside me, and I catch her glancing up often as we walk. We don't really talk, except for the odd question here and there.

When we arrive at the cinema, I see Dane was right. It is crowded. If we don't want to sit right up in the front, we all have to sit separately, but there are a few spots that have two seats available.

"Well, guys, I guess I'll see you at the end of the movie." Parker quickly ushers Addison up the stairs and into two seats right in the middle row. Damn him. I take Elsie's hand and drag her to another two empty seats a few rows up on the side from Parker. I don't even see where Dane and Paislee are.

I settle into my seat and turn to Elsie. "You good? Do you need anything?"

She shakes her head. "No, but I might need your hand throughout the movie if that's okay." She nervously giggles.

"Uh, okay. Why? What movie are we seeing?"

She rolls her beautiful eyes. "Did you not check the ticket?"

"Nope." I shrug.

"It's called *Greta*. It's a scary one." She chews her lip, and I want to kiss it. Seriously, shoot me. I need to tell her the truth. Now.

I open my mouth, about to admit to my lie, when the lights go dim. I rest my arm on the rest and lean over to her and whisper, "You can take my hand anytime you want."

She moves closer, her proximity becoming intoxicating. My heart pounds. This isn't normal for me.

"Okay, just don't tell your girlfriend. I'd hate to cause trouble. We're just friends. Please make sure you tell her that. Crazy friends. Who apparently have dares to complete." Her breath tickles my cheek, and all I can think about is taking her hand.

"Don't worry about that. I want to tell you something when we have a moment."

Elsie leans back and studies me, so I give her a smile. I will tell her as soon as I can. When the time is right.

I can only hope Parker doesn't change his mind and tell Addison in the meantime. I'm sure she would run to Elsie, and then all she will see is me and a great big lie hanging over me like a dark cloud.

CHAPTER
Nine

Elsie

I wonder what Aiden wants to talk to me about. I don't get long to ponder before I'm thrown into the world of a crazy lady who leaves handbags in places, and when people return them, she goes hell crazy, kidnapping them. *Why, oh why, did Addison pick this damn movie?*

I lean closer to Aiden and whisper, "Why did we pick this movie? I'm never returning people's things again. Police station it is."

He laughs and rests his hand on mine. My heart leaps.

"Don't worry… it's all good. You're safe with me." The way he says that tells me something else—I'm not sure what, though. I swear it's been like five minutes and he still hasn't moved his hand. Instead, his grip tightens, and his thumb rubs along my skin, leaving a warm feeling.

Guilt creeps in. I want to pull my hand away, knowing he has a girlfriend, but I'm enjoying his touch and his small caress. Guilt wins, and I reluctantly pull away and go to my bag to dig out the sweets. I can still feel his touch on my skin. There's no way I am going to become the other woman in his life and hurt his girlfriend. I can't do that. It's simply not me.

"Want some?" I offer.

Aiden shakes his head and continues watching the movie. Did I hurt his feelings by pulling my hand away? That felt like a sting to me. I push that feeling aside and stuff another candy in my mouth. Its sweetness dances on my taste buds.

When the movie finally ends, I glance over my shoulder, looking for the others. My mouth falls open at the sight of Paislee and Dane locking lips. I swing back toward Aiden. "Oh my goodness, I just caught Paislee and Dane kissing. Parker is going to flip."

"Are you serious? I could see something was there before the movie even started," he says, casually resting back in his seat.

I grab his shirt, pulling him toward me. "Why didn't you tell me?"

"Because it wasn't my place. That's for them to let everyone know. I'm surprised Parker hasn't noticed. It doesn't take a genius to figure it out," he whispers. *Why is he whispering?*

"I think it's great. They're a cute couple." And now I'm whispering.

The lights haven't fully turned back on in the cinema, and we are so close. I can see his eyes scanning my face.

Abort, Elsie! Abort!

When his eyes rest on my lips, that's my cue to fall back in my chair.

"I mean, I still can't believe it," I quickly keep talking.

Damn, the chemistry between us is heated. I can't allow myself to go there.

Do I like him? Yes.

Does he have a girlfriend? Yes.

Am I willing to break that up? No. Never.

Can I be happy with just being friends? I have to be. That's all it can be.

Aiden stands. "We should go find the others."

I stand and lead the way out of the row of seats. My senses are heightened; I'm so hyperaware of Aiden walking behind me.

On our way down the stairs, Parker, Addison, Dane, and Paislee catch up to us.

"What did you think?" Addison asks.

"Girl, why would you do that to me? I've got to go home tonight and sleep on my own." I'm petrified about being on my own, even though I dorm with another two girls. Addison, I'm sure, will be staying at Parker's tonight, and I'll be left on my own in our dorm room, because the others will be out doing something.

Addison laughs.

They all do, even Aiden.

"Shut up, all of you." I turn to Dane, who's near Paislee, and give him a knowing look, glancing between him and Parker's sister. His eyes widen. I nod. He shuts up right away.

"Why don't you stay at the house and crash on the sofa bed in the living room?" Parker suggests.

"Oh, yes... do that," Addison excitedly agrees.

Do I really want to sleep on a couch that has who-knows-what left on it? These guys have so many sleepovers.

"Is it clean, if you know what I mean?" I ask skeptically.

"No. It's got stains all over it."

My face drops at Parker's words.

"I'm only kidding, Elsie. No one sleeps on it. We bought it before Aiden arrived because we weren't sure about space in the house. So, it's brand new."

Oh, thank goodness. "Okay then. Thanks, guys."

We step out into the night. The boys go in one car, and us girls go with Addison.

On the drive back to the house, I turn around to Paislee. "Where are you staying tonight?"

"She'll most likely be in Dane's bed and then pretend to have been sleeping with you in the morning," Addison voices her thoughts. *I wonder if she meant to say that out loud.*

Paislee's face is one of shock sitting in the back seat.

"How?" she chokes.

"You should really be careful. I saw you both locking lips at the end of the movie."

"Oh, I saw that, too," I say.

"You're not going to tell Parker, are you?" There's fear in Paislee's voice.

Addison answers, "It's not my place to say anything. But know that I don't want to be lying to Parker, either. So, if he asks me, I'll tell him the truth."

"What about you, Elsie?" Paislee asks.

I shake my head. "I'm dealing with my own stuff right

now. I don't have time for someone else's. Your secret's safe with me. Although, Aiden knows as well."

"Are you serious?" Paislee cries.

I turn in my seat to catch her head fall into her hands. "I'm sure he won't say anything. If he was going to, he probably would have already. I don't think he will, though." Aiden doesn't seem like the type to get involved in that kind of stuff.

"Oh, good." She sighs. "But if you get a chance to talk to him privately tonight, can you tell him to keep quiet about it?"

"Yeah, if I get the chance. I'm pretty tired, but I'm not sure I'll be able to sleep after that monstrosity of a movie. It has left me thinking a psycho may burst through the door and kill me at any minute."

We all laugh.

"How are things between you and Aiden?" Addison asks.

I look toward Addison, who gives me a side glance. "There's nothing to tell. He has a girlfriend." I give a fake smile. I'm not going to sit here and tell them how he held my hand or how his closeness affects me in ways I've not experienced before. Trust me to go falling for a guy who's taken.

"What if he didn't have one?" Addison probes.

If only.

"He does and that's it. I'm not going to think about all the what if's when it is what it is right now. He has a girlfriend. I'm happy to get to know him and be his friend." Even as I say the words, I don't believe them. A trickle of sadness creeps in. I'd love for him to not have a girlfriend, but I'm not going to wish her away for my own benefit.

"Long distance doesn't always work," Paislee says.

"And there it is… even if he didn't have a girlfriend, he's still going back to Australia in the future, and then where would we be? I'd be upset, and I'm sure he'd find himself another girl." The car falls silent as I'm sure my tone put out a 'let's not talk about this anymore' vibe.

Move on, Elsie. Stop dwelling on what can or can't be.

Move on.

CHAPTER *Ten*

Aiden

Why the hell didn't I tell her? Damn, I'm such a screw-up. I can hear my sister's voice chewing me out for being so stupid in the first place. And now Elsie's staying at the house. It's like dangling temptation right in my stupid face. I have to tell her tonight.

"Did you guys like the movie?" I ask, pushing away the dread that's filling me.

Parker looks at me in the passenger seat then back to the road. "It wasn't too bad. Addison was pretty jumpy." He chuckles.

"So was Elsie. I thought she was going to have a heart attack in the cinema, the amount of times her hand would clutch at her chest."

Dane is very quiet in the back, and I think Parker notices it as well.

"Was Paislee okay or scared out of her mind?" Parker asks casually, as though he knows nothing. I wonder if he's choosing to be blind to it, or if he actually is oblivious to what's going on between them.

Dane coughs. I smirk, knowing he must feel uncomfortable. "Uh… yeah, she was jumpy as well. She had her hands over her face most of the time." He laughs nervously.

"I hope you were keeping your hands to yourself," Parker teases.

I turn and look at Dane, but his face is unreadable. What seems to be a fake smile pulls at his lips.

"Pfft… of course." Oh, he's good. Wait till the truth is out, though. That's going to be like a bomb exploding. There's no doubt.

"Good. Oi… Aiden, did you talk to Elsie about what I mentioned to you before we went to the movies?" Parker asks.

Damn him. Don't bring that up in the car with Dane. It's like a circle of secrets going on in here.

I rub my neck. "Uh… no. Not yet. Maybe later, since she's staying at the house tonight." The twist in my gut makes me sick.

"Yeah, you better do that."

Silence falls in the car of secrets untold until we get back to the house.

The girls are already there, sitting on the step. Is it possible to feel scared and happy at the same time? I'm happy to be spending more time with Elsie tonight, though

I'm scared about what she's going to say. Like stabbing-pains-to-my-gut scared. How pathetic is that?

We climb out of the car, and the girls stand to greet us.

"G'day, girls," I say.

They all giggle, which is the reaction I was going for.

"It's night, you clown," Elsie cracks back like the little firecracker she is.

"Oh, firecracker, you're a quick one." I wink and stroll past her, purposely moving close, so our arms briefly touch. The tension between us thickens. I have to keep moving, knowing how much her closeness affects me. I have a job to do before I can allow myself to be near her. I shouldn't have held her hand tonight at the movies. I could tell she felt uncomfortable, but I didn't want to let go, though.

"Quick and beautiful…" She rolls her eyes. "Boom! There goes my mouth again," she says.

I can think of one thing I'd like to do with that mouth.

Snap out of it.

I shake my head and head inside the house, following the rest of the gang. I glance at my watch, realizing it's late. We have practice tomorrow. As I think it, Parker says, "Well, guys and gals, we're heading to bed. See you bright and early for practice." He winks and takes Addison's hand and walks away.

Addison stops as they're almost out of the room. "Elsie, the sofa bed is over there. I'm sure Aiden or Dane can help you get it sorted."

"Thanks for leaving me in the lurch," Elsie says sarcastically. I'm sure she knows what's going down in that room tonight.

Addison winks and disappears around into the hallway.

I turn back to the kitchen where Dane and Paislee are pressing against each other.

"You pair better figure your crap out, because I'm not sure how Parker is going to handle this situation," I say in a low voice, gesturing between them as they pull apart, looking sheepish.

I move toward Elsie, who's now at the couch, trying to figure out how to set it up.

"Here. Let me help."

She moves back. "Thanks." Then she looks at Paislee. "He's right… you two do need to figure this out, because Addison knows, so it's only a matter of time before everything is out."

"What do you mean Addison knows?" Dane's panicked eyes flick between Elsie and me.

I raise my hands. "Dude, I said nothing."

"Addison saw you both at the cinema, just like we did," Elsie admits. "You're not being very subtle."

"What she said." I throw my thumb toward Elsie.

"And if you're thinking of sleeping in the same room, you better have a plan of escape." Elsie waves a finger between them both.

Dane takes Paislee's hand and leads her quietly down the hall. *That pair have it bad.*

I pull out the sofa bed and glance up. Elsie is looking toward the hallway. *I wonder what she's thinking.*

Tonight, I'm going to tell her.

She needs to know.

CHAPTER
Eleven

Elsie

I watch Dane and Paislee walk off. She's been on campus for five minutes and has found herself a decent guy. And then there's me, who seems to pick the ones who are just weird, who have girlfriends, and then there are guys like Clifton.

"Oi… are you going to help set this bed up, or am I doing it myself?"

I turn toward Aiden. He's tucking a sheet in around the edges.

"I'm a guest." I hold my arms out. "It's courtesy for the guest to be taken care of." I take a seat on the armrest with a sweet smile plastered across my face.

Aiden shakes his head, but a grin pulls on his lips. "You sure you'll be all right tonight after that movie?" I can hear the mocking in his voice.

Standing, I pull at the sheet to fix up one side. "I'm not a scaredy-cat. I'll survive. I might watch a movie on my phone to get rid of the thought of some crazy lady taking me hostage."

"I can sit out here with you if you want," he offers.

As much as I'd love for him to sit in the bed with me, I worry what might happen if he did. "No, it's okay," I quickly reply. The words taste foreign as I speak them, because I desperately want him to stay out here with me. But I know if he does, I will probably say the wrong thing, and then we'll be left with awkwardness between us. I doubt he even sees that I'm interested in him.

"Just for a little while."

I'm about to answer when I remember something. "Hey, you mentioned you needed to talk to me?" I reach up and pull my hair tie out and let my long brown hair fall over my shoulders. I turn to Aiden, and he's watching me hungrily. I snap my fingers.

Aiden blinks a few times then straightens up. "Sorry, I drifted off for a moment. What did you say?" He runs his hand through his hair.

"You wanted to tell me something earlier."

He moves around to where I'm standing. His hands lift and rest on my shoulders. My chest tightens. *What is he doing?* Suddenly, he gives me a light shove, and I'm tumbling back onto the sofa bed with a laugh.

"What was that for?"

He shrugs. "Just because."

I pull my phone from my back pocket and then fix my

pillow and sit up. I watch as Aiden slips his shoes off then climbs over my legs and settles in beside me.

"Are you all right there?" I ask, raising my eyebrows with some amusement in my tone.

"Yep." He slides a little closer, his arm against mine. *What is he playing at?* It's as if he's doing this on purpose.

"Hey, have you spoken to your girlfriend lately?" I decide to bring up the inevitable. I recall Addison mentioning tonight about him having a fake girlfriend. What if he's been lying to me? I've never seen him on the phone to her, and he hasn't shown me a picture.

His mouth flattens. "No, we… ah… decided to have a break."

I can't help my reaction. My mouth falls open, and my eyes widen. "Oh, no. Really? Are you okay?" I'm not sure what to do or say. Should I give him a hug, hold his hand, or do nothing?

Clearing his throat, he says, "Yeah, I'm okay. It was for the best." His gaze doesn't shift from his phone.

"I'm here if you ever need to talk," I reply softly.

Then his eyes meet mine.

I could easily lean over and kiss those pink lips. They're so inviting. Enticing.

"Thanks. Did you want to watch a movie on the iPad?" he asks, changing the subject rather quickly.

I put my phone down beside me. "Yeah, okay, but no scary movies."

He laughs. "No."

Aiden sets the iPad up between us. I wriggle in under the blankets and turn on my side toward the iPad. Aiden has chosen a *Star Wars* movie.

"I've not seen any of these movies," I say as I pull the pillow under my head to get more comfortable. Looking up, I'm met with an Aiden whose mouth is open, clearly shocked.

"You've never watched *Star Wars?*"

I shake my head.

"Well, we better go back to the very first one. The way they've made these movies is a little all over the place, but we'll watch *The Phantom Menace.*"

"How many are there?"

"There are eight movies, all intertwined, and then there are two extras where they give you the backstory of characters and pivotal moments to the main movies." His finger slides down on the other side of the screen, and he changes the movie.

"I'll shut the lights off," I say then start to get up.

"No, it's okay. The boys have Alexa. Hey, Alexa, turn lights off."

I wait, and the room goes black. Aiden's face is lit only by the iPad.

"Wow! I've heard about these but have never seen one in use. They must have only just got that."

"I bought it when I first arrived. I've gotten everything set up, so now we can shut the lights off out here by just saying the words. I have a similar thing at home."

"Wow! I'm not a tech-savvy person. I know how to use simple programs on my computer, and give me a phone, I'm a champion. They should make texting an Olympic sport. I'm sure I'd take a gold medal out on that one." I lift my head and pull my hair out from under me, flicking it behind me to keep it out of my way.

"I'm sure my sister could give you a run for your money." He chuckles.

"I bet any fifteen-year-old could. The way they eat up

technology these days. I see little toddlers in carts at the shops, watching their parents' phones. It's crazy. I'm sure I'd do it for my kids to just get a little peace and quiet." I laugh.

"Kids would be hard work."

"Agreed."

The movie is ready to go, and I wait for him to hit play. "Are you ready to dive into the awesome world of *Star Wars?* You will love it."

I cock my eyebrow. "I'll be the judge of that."

Reaching down, he hits play, and for the next couple of hours, I'm swallowed up in a world of a young boy, weird-looking creatures, crazy languages, and fighting scenes with light sticks.

At the end, the credits start rolling, and I glance over at Aiden, who's passed out. I look at the time on the iPad— it's three in the morning. Damn, I'm going to be tired tomorrow.

I turn off the screen and slip his iPad on the floor with my phone. I leave Aiden where he is, not wanting to disturb him. Instead, I roll over with my back to him. Every part of me is highly aware he's there.

He's *single* now. Well, on a break.

Even if I end up tangled over him through the night, at least now I've got no reason to feel guilty.

CHAPTER Twelve

Elsie

Heat presses against my back, and a weight over my waist startles me awake. My eyes widening, I shuffle slightly.

"Go back to sleep." That accent pulls me out of the panic which was starting to settle in. Then, I remember last night.

"Get off me," I grumble, shoving him backward.

I roll over onto my back while Aiden stretches. He slept on top of the blankets. As he lifts his arms above his head, his shirt raises, showing me that V which causes me to bite my lip. Damn!

"What's the time?" he asks.

Lifting my arm, I rub my eyes and squint at my watch.

"It's seven-thirty."

Aiden leaps off the bed and takes off down the hallway, cursing along the way.

"What's wrong?" I ask, sitting up.

Aiden sits back on the bed, now dressed in his basketball gear, and pulls his shoes on. "I'm late for practice."

I furrow my brows and purse my lips. "On a Sunday?"

Then he stops. His head drops, and laughter leaves his mouth. "Gee, don't I feel stupid. Those fellas played me."

I smile. "Yep, I bet you do."

He turns. "You wanna go grab breakfast?"

I nod. "Sure. Why not?" I reply, secretly trying to compose myself so I don't leap up and cheer.

He actually wants to spend time with me.

Me…

We walk toward the campus café, my place of work, which reminds me I need to check my hours for next week.

"So, what are you studying?" Aiden asks.

The sun heats my back as we walk. I turn to him. "I want to help special needs kids. So, kind of like a speech therapist or occupational therapist. My mother wants me to be a doctor"—I screw up my nose—"or something professional like that." The word doctor rolls off my tongue like a foul taste.

"What's that about? You don't seem too impressed with what your mother wants."

I shrug. "Since she's a single mom, and she's slaved away at job after job to get me into college, she feels it's her place to dictate what I study. I guess that's why my brother has chosen to travel and keep his distance."

"That must be hard," he says as he turns toward me.

"It is what it is. There have been plenty of fights and arguments over what I want to study. With every phone call I get from Mom, she has mastered how to make me feel guilty, even though I'm a straight-A student and pass all my classes. It somehow doesn't feel like it's enough for her." Aiden remains silent. "Anyway, enough about me and my drama. What about you? What are your plans with school and travel?"

"I don't really have a plan. I'm enrolled in this college for the semester, and then I will decide if I should move on to another place or stay." He sighs, running his fingers through his hair. "I also know what it's like to have a parent who thinks they own the kind of person you're going to become… My dad wants me to take over the family business."

"Oh yeah? What's the family business?"

"Let's see. He's a lawyer, his father was a lawyer, and his father…" he trails off. "You catchin' my drift here?"

"Oh, so he wants you to be a lawyer?" She laughs sarcastically.

Aiden nods. "Yeppers, and I'm not overly interested in doing that. I'm all for extreme sports and sports in general. I don't care much for the stress of being what they want me to be." His voice becomes low and void of his usual happy self.

"Does it make you angry?"

"Not so much angry… more annoyed. My father didn't want me to come here, because if I'm here, then he can't run my life or the schooling I want to do. I want to experience everything and be happy." Aiden looks up to the blue sky and takes a deep breath.

"I understand. If I could do things like what you're

doing, I would. I guess that's why I don't back down from dares. They push me out of my comfort zone. They give me an opportunity to experience things on a different level."

Aiden takes my hand and stops. My heart rate spikes, and I stare down at our locked hands, then back up to his face. His beautiful features hold my attention and bring butterflies to my stomach.

"So, you keen to do the cliff jump?"

My stomach plummets to the ground beneath me, all good feelings now gone. "I'll admit, I'm petrified, like to the point where it makes me feel sick with anxiety." I laugh nervously.

He squeezes my hand. "Let's start with the easier of the two dares. Fishing?"

My nose screws up. "I've been fishing once before, and it wasn't much fun. In fact, it was boring."

"You acted as though you hadn't been the other night when I put it to you."

"There's a lot you don't know about me, Aussie guy." I give him a wry smile while waggling my eyebrows at him. "And I bet you thought you had gotten me."

Aiden steps closer, shoulders squared, and his face staring down at me. Heavy eyes stir up the butterflies in my stomach again. "Oh, I'm sure I could read you like a book, you firecracker. One day, I'll get you in a dare that's going to cause you to lose your breath."

I laugh. "What does that even mean?"

His thumb moves over my knuckles. "You'll find out soon enough."

Aiden steps back and releases my hand, but I want him to keep hold of it. I want his lips pressed to mine. I want to taste him. Only I don't think that's going to happen.

When we get to the café, Addison is working. Walking up to the counter, I say, "I didn't even hear you leave this morning."

"I didn't want to disturb the canoodling that was happening on the sofa bed." She laughs, waggling her eyebrows at us.

Aiden clears his throat. I turn to him as he rubs the back of his neck.

"Anyway…" I draw out the word. "I'm going to check my hours for next week. I'll have the big breakfast and an orange juice." I step around the counter and make my way to the small office out back. I'm flicking through the schedule when Addison comes skipping—actually skipping—into the office.

Her hands are clenched together at her chest, and a massive toothy grin is plastered across her face. "Well, well, well… you pair looked cozy this morning." She jumps up and down excitedly.

Rolling my eyes, I say, "Don't read too much into it. He's just broken up with his girlfriend, apparently."

"Are you serious? Why aren't you happy about this?" she whispers.

I nod. "That's what he told me last night. A part of me wonders if it's because of me. It all seems so sudden." I finally find my page and grab a piece of blank paper from the desk and scribble my hours down.

"It's his choice, and he's not going to be here for long." She pauses for a second then continues, "So, are you going to pursue anything?" she asks, a little too excited. *This girl doesn't give up.*

"I don't know. He's leaving eventually. I'll just end up with my heart broken." I'm not ready for a broken heart. I've always been the heartbreaker. The one-night stand. The one to walk away first. I'm not sure I could do that with Aiden.

Addison steps closer. "You can't let the fear of him leaving stop you from giving it a go. Have a little fun, girl. Stop worrying about tutoring and all that other stuff and just do you for once. I did and look where that's gotten me." She winks.

"Yeah, yeah," I respond dryly and move around her.

She's right. To wear my heart on my sleeve is a whole new thing for me. I'm just not sure I'm ready to open myself up to Aiden.

I find Aiden sitting at a table outside. I pause before going out to him. His eyes are bright. I watch them dance as he looks around him, taking in the campus atmosphere before him. He's so full of life and wants to explore and do things I'd probably only dream of doing—like jumping off a damn cliff. I would never have chosen to do that in a million years, and now I've gotten myself into this, and I can't pull out.

He leans back in his chair and crosses his arms over his chest. The muscles in his arms stand out and are so defined. I want those arms wrapped around me.

A throat clears behind me. Spinning, I catch Addison giving me a knowing grin, so I shake my head.

Turning back to Aiden, his eyes are on me.

Caught...

CHAPTER Thirteen

Aiden

Elsie and Addison have been gone for a while. I notice the other chick is at the counter serving. Taking my seat at one of the few tables outside, I watch the other students flow in and out of the café and then run off to study or do who knows what. The schooling here is so different from back home in Australia. It's so much more laid-back, but there are also serious people who genuinely want to learn, and then there are the ones who want to party all the time.

A sense of being watched hits me. Turning around, I catch sight of Elsie, only she's not watching me. She's facing Addison, who appears to be laughing. Elsie turns back my way. A small smile kicks up her light-pink lips. The rhythm in my chest skips a beat. I sit a little higher in my chair. Elsie shakes her head slightly and heads toward our table.

I grab my orange juice and take a large gulp.

She pulls out a chair and slides in. Her floral perfume rushes my way, and I inhale her scent, causing a twist to my stomach. She's obviously borrowed spray from Addison, considering she hasn't gone anywhere to refresh.

I push the other orange juice toward her. "For you…"

Her head lifts, and our eyes connect. "Thanks. How much do I owe you?" She goes to dig in the small brown bag she has hanging over her shoulder.

"No, you don't owe me anything. My shout. Next time, you can get it."

Elsie looks up, studies me. "Okay. Next time, my shout."

Silence falls between us as she takes a sip of her juice, so I try to think of something to say.

"How long have Addison and Parker been together?" I ask.

Her brow furrows as though she's thinking on my question. "It hasn't been long. To be honest, I've not kept track, but it's really only new." She shrugs. "So, tell me what happened with you and your girlfriend?"

The dread I'd thought would go once I removed my fake girlfriend from the scene comes back like somebody has swung a bat at my stomach. My eyes drop, and I quickly pick up my cup and take another drink.

I can see her watching me from the corner of my eye. *Can she see through the lie I've created?* Finally, I answer. "Just… ah… wanted different things." I stumble over my words. Even I don't believe myself by the way I sound. With a trembling hand, I pick up my glass and down another mouthful of my drink. In my haste, the mouthful goes down all wrong, and I start coughing. My lungs want to jump out of my throat. I take a small sip of my drink, trying to stop it.

When I glance up, Elsie has tears streaming down her face.

"Shut up," I grumble but give her a smile.

More laughter follows. "Oh, my goodness. So funny." She sighs, wiping her face. Her eyes glisten and stare right at me. I know, right in this moment, that if she ever finds out the truth about my apparent girlfriend, she'll hate me. I'm not sure I could handle that. No other girl has taken a hold of my heart like Elsie has. There's something about her which captures my undivided attention.

"No, it's not. I could have died. Choking on my damn juice."

More laughter and I follow suit. Her happiness is infectious. After a moment, our mirth subsides, and we're left in silence. Our food is brought out moments later, and we begin digging in. I didn't realize how damn hungry I was until now, only I'm not just hungry for food. I catch Elsie putting a forkful into her mouth. The way her lips move— oh hell. I suck in my bottom lip and bite it, holding back a groan. Damn!

"Everything okay with the food?"

I snap out of my trance and turn toward Addison, who's standing beside the table.

"Always good," Elsie says with food still in her mouth. She's not a Miss Proper-Girl like the others I've met since being here. That Stacey chick is high maintenance.

"Don't choke on your food." Addison laughs then turns to me. "Is everything all right?"

"Yep."

Her eyebrows raise, and I think I've been caught staring at Elsie. My eyes go back to my plate, and I shove more food in my mouth.

"What are you guys planning to do today?" Addison asks.

I shrug and look at Elsie.

"Not sure. I have tutoring emails to catch up on and homework to finish. What about you, Aiden?"

I glance between them. "Uhh… I was going to take you fishing." I cock my eyebrow. Hers raise, and her mouth forms an *O* shape.

"Sure, I'm keen. Do you have stuff for fishing?"

I hear the tone of her voice which says, *"You don't have anything prepared for fishing."*

"We'll make a quick stop at the shop and grab a few things. There's no way you're getting out of this."

"Okay, but I already told you I've been fishing before. Can't say I'm great at it, though." She laughs.

"That's okay. I'm sure Aiden here will be happy to lend a hand," Addison responds and winks at me.

I'm not sure what Addison is playing at. "Sure, of course, I'll help. Let's finish up here, and we'll go get a couple of things."

"Excellent. I look forward to hearing about it." Addison claps then turns and leaves us.

"Is she always this much of a sticky beak?"

"A what?"

"A person who likes to stick their nose into other people's business."

"Oh, she isn't usually. But perhaps when it comes to me, she likes to know what's going on." She downs the last of her drink and pushes her plate away from her. She's demolished her food and I'm still going.

This girl isn't like any other I have ever met.

CHAPTER
Fourteen

Elsie

This isn't how I saw my day turning out. Yet, here I am, at a popular fishing spot on the wharf. There are only three other people around, and I'm sure they think we're a joke and aren't serious about catching anything. I don't even have high hopes of reeling a fish in, but I am happy to be here with Aiden.

I watch him place the tackle box and rods he bought on the wooden wharf. He takes a seat on the edge while I stand there and gawk at him. His reasonably tight sky-blue shirt moves with his muscles, and his arms flex as he twists and grabs the first fishing rod.

"Are you going to sit?" he asks while digging through the box and opening the little packets full of sinkers, hooks, and lures.

I step up and take a seat beside him. He leans into me, gently brushing himself against me. My heart rate spikes, and a shiver runs all the way down my spine. I glance down at my watch—ten a.m. I wonder how long Aiden plans to stay here.

"You already planning your escape?" He shoves my shoulder slightly.

I face him. His brown eyes shine. My stomach flutters. I have to remind myself that he's just had his heart broken by ending it with his girlfriend and most likely isn't looking for a new relationship right now.

"Nope, was just checking the time. I do really have tutoring to catch up on, but that can wait till later. Hey, did you find yourself a tutor?" I'd meant to ask him sooner. I didn't see his name appear on my list, so I assume he went with another tutor.

He focuses on tying a knot around a sinker—I think that's what they're called. "Yeah, I did, just waiting to hear back."

I nod. The little ache in my heart settles there. *Why didn't he ask me?* "What is it you're working on?"

Aiden looks up, his brow furrowed. "It's a *Romeo and Juliet* thing for English. We have to write a modernized letter about love. I'm not the greatest with English."

"Yeah, that Australian language is hard to pick up." I laugh.

"Whatever. You understand me. I've not had you ask me to repeat anything. I've been very conscious of my word choices to make sure you understand what I'm trying to say."

"Oh, aren't you thoughtful," I respond dryly. His accent, though, is enough for him to have all the girls flocking to him, and I can't blame them.

Aiden stands and places a piece of bait on the hook he's just finished tying. "All right, this rod is yours. Do you know how to cast?"

"How about you do this one for me?" *I wonder how many times I can get him to do it for me?* I laugh to myself.

He moves the rod until it's hanging behind him. In one swift move, he flicks it out, then it drops into the water, then he does a maneuver and turns something off the reel. I'm so not a fishing person. I don't even eat seafood, but I'm willing to do this to get to know Aiden. Plus, he did dare me, and at least I'm not jumping off a cliff right now.

Aiden hands me the fishing rod. Our fingers touch, and I try not to show my reaction. My body electrifies from one small touch. "Here. Just keep your finger on the line to feel for bites. Wait until they start pulling and then reel it in," he instructs.

I settle in on the side of the wharf. He sets up the other rod and throws the line out like he did with mine. With a deep sigh, he takes a seat beside me again.

"Do you do this back home?" I ask as I stare out at the ocean.

"Yeah. My parents have a boat we take out as often as we can. You should see the kinds of fish we've caught while far out in the ocean. My dad caught a small shark once."

My head flicks toward him. "Really? A shark?"

He nods, smiling.

"And that's why I would hate going to Australia. You have all these creepy crawlies that just freak me the hell out. Huge spiders, deadly snakes, and who knows what else is hiding over there ready to eat me."

Aiden laughs, throwing his head back. "It's not a scary place. Dude, you have bears around here. You're overreacting. I'll protect you if you ever travel to Australia." He taps his hand on my leg, and immediately, goose bumps rise over my skin.

"Yeah… when I *eventually* come to Australia," I say sarcastically. "That won't happen."

"Why not?"

I shrug, turning to him. "I feel like there's pressure for me to finish college and get a good job. You know, make money. It seems to be the normal thing to do. Well, that's what my mother expects me to do. If I don't, then guilt eats away at me because I'm not doing what my mother expects of me. I already feel guilty because I'm not studying what she wants me to."

Aiden's lips form a thin line, then he shrugs. "I think you need to find a balance. You have to find what sets your heart on fire. What's the point in this life if we aren't going to enjoy it? There are so many people who don't live, and when a terrible thing happens, or they get sick, they decide then that they must do something to make themselves happy. Live in the now. There are traveling bloggers who make money."

Aiden's words cause me to turn to him. "You sound like you're speaking from experience when you talk about a person getting sick or something?"

He fiddles with the fishing rod, then his head rises, and I can see the pain in his eyes as he looks out to the bright-blue ocean. "Yeah…" He pauses then continues, "My best friend died from leukemia."

"Oh, I'm so sorry, Aiden." Raising my hand, I reach over and gently rub his leg, just a friendly gesture. As I lift my hand to remove it, he takes it and places it back on his leg. Only, he doesn't let it go. My chest swells.

"It's okay. I guess that's why I'm so out there and trying to live my life. I saw how quickly his deteriorated. He was such a happy-go-lucky guy who could make anyone smile. The day he lost his fight, a light went out in my life. I felt it. It was the worst kind of feeling in the world. You don't understand true loss until it's a friend or family member. I grew up with Tom. We'd been best mates since we started in first grade. Our mums soon realized that we were inseparable, and they became great friends as well—still are to this day."

A tear slips down my cheek. I let it. I don't care if he sees it as I stare out at the ocean. The way the breeze kisses my damp cheek and the waves dance into the shore is peaceful. My hand is released, and Aiden brushes away my tears.

"I'm sorry." I bring my hand back and swipe away the tear on the other side of my face. His words hit me right in the chest, because I've never known true loss like he has. Well, not yet, anyway.

"You've got nothing to be sorry about. I'm okay to talk about Tom. It's because of him I'm here."

"How so?"

"It's been twelve months since he passed away, and we were both going to travel. Two crazy Australian boys with only our dreams carrying us across different countries. We'd been saving since we got our first jobs in high school." He clears his throat as if moving his emotions from there. "When Tom passed away, he left his savings to me." He takes a large breath. "Of all people, me. His family are well off, just like mine, and so his parents had no issues giving me the money, but they felt like I needed to do something worthy with it. So, I've stuck to our dream. This is only the beginning of a year-long travel I plan to do."

I take a deep breath. "Wow." I sigh. "That's beautiful. You're keeping the memory of your friend alive." I turn to him, catching him nodding. "You and he must have had a great friendship."

"We did. It was always me and Tom. When it came to girls, we had each other's back and made sure we didn't date crazy chicks."

I laugh. So does he, and that's when I feel a small tug on my line.

"Oh, I think a fish is biting," I whisper. "I am not sure why I'm whispering, though. Perhaps I don't want to scare away whatever's biting on my line." I look to Aiden for advice.

The line tugs again while the top of the rod bends.

"If you get another one like that, pull back and then start reelin' it in." His body has turned toward me. I can feel the heat of his stare boring into me.

Then, there's a bigger bite and tug, so I do what he said. I yank back, and there's possibly a fish on the end, pulling against my line.

"Start windin' it in."

Grabbing the reel, I pull then wind and pull then wind.

"It looks like a decent size, whatever it is. Keep goin.'"

I pull again, then the weight that was there a moment ago suddenly disappears, and my entire body flies back. I can't help but break out in laughter.

I'm lying back on the wood, laughing, my stomach tighter with each giggle. I place the rod beside me with tears falling down my cheeks. Usually, I'd be totally embarrassed by something like this, but I couldn't care less, especially not in front of Aiden, for some reason.

"You okay?" He places his rod down and leans over to offer me a hand. I take it, and he pulls me up. We were close before, but now we're a hair's breadth apart. My laughing stops, but the smile doesn't move from my face. My heart jumps at our closeness. Our eyes burn into each other's. His eyes shift from mine to my lips and back up again. Heat pools in my stomach.

Aiden inches closer. I close my eyes as he nears and feel the warmth of his soft lips lightly brushing over mine.

I want more.

I open my eyes and reach up, gently rubbing my hand on his cheek then dropping it back to my lap. He must take that as an invitation, and within seconds, his mouth is back on mine. Only this time, he's not so gentle. Our lips move with such rhythm we could be writing our own song. His hands move and take my face, and when he does, goose bumps spread over my body like a wildfire.

After a moment, he pulls away, but I want those lips back. I stare at him. His eyes blaze with emotion, and it slaps me in the face. Our breaths are heavy, and I'm sure if we weren't in public, more would happen.

"Wow," I breathe. I've been wanting to do that since I met him, and it was even better than I imagined.

"Sorry. I couldn't help myself," he says with a kind softness to his voice.

I reach out and place my hand on his neck. "It was… perfect."

He grins when the words leave my lips. "I can't promise it won't happen again." His hand reaches up and takes mine from his neck.

"That's okay. I'm sure I can survive another kiss like that one."

"How about multiple?" He waggles his eyebrows.

"Oh, I don't know. You might run away with my heart. It's already trying to escape." The pounding music in my chest hasn't settled since we sat down.

The way he has this invisible hold over me is something I probably should be scared of.

Because when he eventually leaves, I'm sure he'll have one extra piece of baggage he takes along with him—my heart.

CHAPTER Fifteen

Aiden

I want to hold her in my arms and take her away—travel together. The way her gaze holds mine, it's as if there are a thousand stories sitting behind them, a thousand secrets she wants to share, and I'd be happy to sit here and listen to every single one. The kiss was unplanned. Those peach-pink lips were soft as feathers against mine, and it makes me want more.

Elsie picks up the rod and reels in the rest of the line then places it down again. "I think I'm done with fishing for today." She shrugs. "I'm happy to stay and wait for you to catch something if you want."

"Sure. Why not? I've got all this bait to use up." In all honesty, I want to spend more time with her, and if we have to sit here and fish, then I am all for it. Hearing her laughter brings a smile to my face every single time. Talking to her is easy. I didn't think I'd bring Tom up to her—or anyone— over here. It always hurts too much, so I barely mention him. It's been a year, and I miss my friend so much. I've never been close to anyone like that since. I guess I'm afraid that they'll leave me. It's a stupid thought, really.

"So, you're here for the semester, and where are you planning to go after that?" Elsie asks as I slip more bait onto my hook.

I take a moment to think about her question. "I really don't know. I'll find somewhere, I'm sure of it, and I've got a bit of time to think about it. I may end up hanging around."

Elsie cocks an eyebrow. "Really? You'd hang around here when you've got the rest of the world to discover?" I can hear the shock in her words.

Flicking the rod out, I settle it between my legs once again before I answer. Little does she know that it's because of her I wouldn't mind hanging around. "Yeah. I've got a good group of friends around me here." I face her.

"But the whole thing was your pact to travel. Why would you stop that? You could easily come back after you're done visiting places you want to go."

"Aren't having friends important, though?"

"Well, yes, but you came all this way to see the world. Don't stop in this little town. Go explore. There's so much more for you to do. More friends for you to make."

Damn! It almost sounds as though she's trying to push me away.

I give her a side glance. "Are you trying to get rid of me?"

She straightens her back. "What? No. I just think you've come so far, and you need to do what you and your friend were planning. It's his legacy." Her voice softens as she says the last part of her argument.

"Come with me then?" The words are out before I can stop myself.

What the hell am I thinking?

Her mouth hangs open. She's speechless. I reach over and touch her chin, and her mouth snaps shut. Still, she says nothing, but then she seems to regain her senses and says, "I know you're only joking, so don't tempt me." She laughs it off.

I'd love for her to travel with me. Having her with me would be so much fun. Seeing the world together. "Who says I'm joking?"

"Yeah, nice try." She faces the ocean, breaking our intense stare. "Anyway, what are your plans for the rest of the day?"

I don't even need to think about this, so I answer, "To spend it with you."

Pink flushes her cheeks. Without thinking, I grab her hand from where it's resting on her leg. Her gaze drops to where our hands are locked together. I wonder what she's thinking. *Was this what she wanted to happen?*

That kiss, though. It spoke volumes. The way she responded tells me she's willing for something or she would have pushed me away. Wouldn't she? Sometimes she's easy to read, and other times, like now, I'm so unsure.

Elsie squeezes my hand, and the small bit of uncertainty I had swimming around in my gut tells me she's okay. Well, I hope so.

"So, tell me, can you play basketball?" I remember how she had been super keen to play the first—well, technically, the second—time we met.

A nervous cough-slash-laugh bubbles up from her throat. "That would be a no. I have no idea." She laughs. "I was trying to impress you." Elsie nudges my shoulder without turning toward me. She impressed me all right.

"You definitely made yourself unforgettable." I chuckle then receive another nudge, only this time, much harder.

"Shut up," she snaps, but she's still playful.

"And you totally collected your head on the way out." More laughter erupts between us.

"I was trying to impress you. It obviously worked if you're sitting here with me now." Elsie turns my way. Her shining eyes burn into mine. Her beautiful pink skin lights up under the sun. Her flushed cheeks make my hand ache to reach out and touch her, to glide my fingers down her smooth skin.

"How could I forget when you were trying to escape as fast as you could. I was impressed with how you handled yourself."

Elsie rolls her eyes. "Stop making fun of me."

"I'm going to teach you a little basketball before I leave. I *dare* you to let me teach you." I throw down the gauntlet, knowing she can't pass up a dare. *Thanks, Addison, for filling me in on that little fact.*

Elsie is silent a moment before answering, "Okay, that's pretty easy. Surely, it's not that hard to learn basics."

"Who said anything about basics?" I tease. I want to get a rise out of her.

"Oh, come on… I'm not a super sporty girl. Nothing like Addison, anyway. Yes, I dress as though I've gone to the gym, but it's only a front. I just love wearing tights and tees."

"Let me say, I love you in tights." I give her a half-smile.

"Calm down there, mister." She releases my hand and taps my shoulder then shakes her head.

"One more thing. I *dare* you to kiss me again." I watch and wait for her reaction.

She gives me nothing.

I wait longer.

Elsie slowly leans over with a small grin on her face, but I quickly close the space, sealing another kiss on her lips. *I could kiss her all day.*

When she pulls back, the smile on her face is bright. "That one was easy." She winks.

I shake my head, chuckling.

We spend the rest of the morning and afternoon on the wharf. I love spending time with her. We make each other laugh, and it feels good. I have so many opportunities to tell her the truth about my *fake girlfriend,* but I don't. It should all be okay now that I've apparently ended things with her anyway, so why bother telling her the 'actual' truth. There's no need to go down that path.

It's wrong and I know it, but I don't want to hurt her.

When I get back to the house, Parker's sitting in the living room. The sofa bed's all packed away. I head to the fridge to make a sandwich.

"So, Addison tells me that you ended things with your *girlfriend?*" He's not impressed—at all. The way the words come out so dry, it's as if they have rolled across the desert to get to me. It instantly burns me.

Stopping what I'm doing, I turn, and his features are stone. "Yeah…" I draw out the word, unsure what else to say.

Parker rises from the couch. "You should've been honest

with her. What are you doing?" Oh hell, I can tell he's pissed off. "You're building a friendship based on a lie."

I nod. Unease settles in the pit of my stomach. It makes me ill. "I know. I will tell her the truth."

Parker folds his arms across his chest and stares me down. "You're going to break her heart. You've got to see that. And in turn, I'm lying to Addison, which I hate. If she finds out that I knew about this from the start, I'm going to be in trouble. None of this sits right with me."

"I know. I know. I'm sorry. I'll fix it."

"You better, or I'm going to tell Addison, and she'll surely fill Elsie in on this lie. Just tell the damn truth before you break both of the girls' hearts."

"Both girls?"

"Yeah. It'll break Addison's heart as well because she likes you."

I hang my head. The shame pumps through my veins. "Okay. I'll fix this. But what if she hates me after I tell her?"

Parker smirks. "She's going to be angry. Both of them will, there is no doubt. But you have to prove to them that you're not that person. You're a good person, Aiden. Unfortunately, you've done a stupid thing."

I nod, and Parker exits the room.

I've screwed up.

How am I meant to fix this without Elsie hating me?

CHAPTER
Sixteen

Elsie

Spending yesterday with Aiden had been great, and those kisses were memorable. Addison wasn't at the dorm when I arrived home, so I managed to catch up on my homework and schedule out my week with tutoring. Sitting in my bedroom at my desk, I check my watch to make sure I'm not going to be late to my first class of the day. Sweet. I have an hour to spare.

I click open my emails and clear anything that's not needed. Stupid spam. Then, I proceed to check the junk folder. There are always emails in there that shouldn't be from students who need tutoring.

There are three emails. Clicking them open one by one and then moving them to the inbox, I glance over the last one. There's no name to tell me who it's from, except when I open it, it's signed off with an *A*. I purse my lips, thinking a moment. *Could this be Aiden?* Surely, he would just ask me for help, or if he was trying to remain a secret, he'd be a little more ingenious about it.

Okay, buddy. Two can play this game.

I click open the attachment, and it's the English assignment we received in class last week about Shakespeare. We've got to write a meaningful poem, taking inspiration from Shakespearian plays. It's probably one of the most straightforward assignments this term. *Why would Aiden need help?*

I click reply.

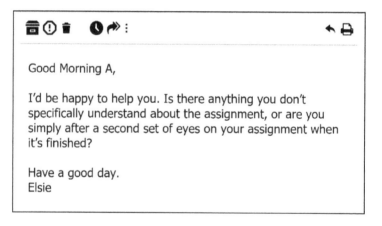

Good Morning A,

I'd be happy to help you. Is there anything you don't specifically understand about the assignment, or are you simply after a second set of eyes on your assignment when it's finished?

Have a good day.
Elsie

I close down my email and grab the last of my books for class. I have to work tonight for Addison because she has a date with Parker. My phone rings, and for a moment, I stare at the name—Mom. I'm sure she's going to ruin my mood, but I slide my finger to answer anyway.

"Hey, Mom." I try to sound happy to hear from her, but it's hard.

"Hey, Elsie. How are you? I haven't heard from you in a

little while, so I was checking in to see how things are going?" I hear something banging around in the background on her end.

"Nothing new to report here, Mom. I've been busy with classes and tutoring. You know me, nose in my books." I pick up a pen and start scribbling on a notebook, but it's simply doodles.

"I heard a rumor you are hanging around with an Australian boy. Is this true?" Damn Mom and her friends. *I wonder who saw me this time.*

"He's a friend, Mom." I sigh. Dropping my pen, I lift my hand to rub my forehead, trying to relieve some tension.

"He's a distraction." Her words sting.

I snap, "Why are you so against me having a life? Am I not allowed to have friends? To go experience the world?" My voice rises with each word. I pick the pen up again and toss it hard against the wall. It smashes and tinkles to the floor.

"Excuse me?"

"You heard me. I love you, Mom, and I appreciate all you've done for me, but… I'm old enough to make my own decisions when it comes to what I want to study. I'm a good student and pass all my classes. I help other students pass their classes as a tutor. Can't you be happy for me? Show some support instead of making me feel guilty over every little thing I do." My lip comes between my teeth and I bite, stopping myself from continuing and sounding like an ungrateful daughter.

There's silence on the end of the phone.

After a second, I hear a sniffle.

"Mom, are you okay? I didn't mean to hurt your feelings."

"No, no, you're right. I simply want you to be the best

you can be. Which is why I push like I d-do." Her voice cracks, and I already know there are tears falling down her face.

"I know, Mom, but you make me feel like everything I'm doing is wrong. You've done it for years. I don't say this to hurt you. I've not said anything to you before because you're my mom, and I hate hurting your feelings." Guilt builds in my chest. I feel like such a terrible daughter talking to her this way. I'm not even sure what's gotten into me. Perhaps spending time with Aiden has given me some bravado to stand up for the things I'd like to do in my life. He's doing things for his best friend, living the life they wanted to live together. I want a life like that.

"Thank you for telling me, Elsie. I'm sorry for being one of those parents who cares too much." And there it is! I'm not even sure she realizes she's doing it now.

"Mom, you're doing it again," I respond dryly.

I hear a shuffle on the end of the line. "Sorry, honey. I promise it's something I'll work on. You're a great daughter. You're so smart. I know you'll make the right decisions for you, and I'll be here to offer you the support and advice you need when you want it."

Wow! Why didn't I have this conversation with her when I first started college?

"Thank you, Mom. I love you, and you have no idea how much I appreciate all you've done and still do for me." A lump catches in my throat.

"I love you, too, Elsie. I'll let you get back to whatever it is you were doing."

"I wasn't doing much, just about to head out the door."

"I'll talk to you later, darling."

you're good at that. Just be yourself." She shakes me a little, and I laugh.

"All right. I'll try. No falling for the Aussie guy. Right?"

"Yes! That's right. No falling."

It's already too late, because I am falling. I'm teetering on the edge of a waterfall right now, and if Aiden tells me he has feelings for me, I know I will leap right off. Falling headfirst.

Will it hurt? Yes.

Am I going to get my heart broken? It's a high possibility, but I need to take a chance. I will take that chance on Aiden even if he is leaving.

"Okay, I have to head out if I'm going to make it to class on time." I screw up my nose. "And you need to shower." I laugh, my hand coming up to hold my nose.

Addison shoves me playfully. "Shut up! I'll see you later. Thanks again for covering for me tonight."

"That's okay. I need the hours."

We say our goodbyes, and I go straight for the café. I stare down at my phone, typing out a message to Willow and Jane when an arm drops over my shoulder. The familiar musk scent makes my heart rate spike. I flick my head up, and I'm greeted with a perfect smile. *Do not fall.* I remind myself of the lie I am trying to sell to myself.

"Hey there, firecracker."

"Firecracker, eh? Are we going to go with that?" I hit send on my message and then shove my phone in my back pocket.

"It suits you." He pulls me tighter against him.

I sigh silently, relishing in his warmth and touch. Addison's words from earlier ring through my mind. *He's only just ended a relationship.*

Don't fall…

I'm trying. Only when he's this close to me and makes my heart smile, how can I not?

"Thanks," I reply, clipped, annoyed at myself for letting Addison ruin my happy moment.

"Hey, did you want to come around tonight and watch the second movie of *Star Wars?*" His hip bumps mine.

"I don't think I can. I have to fill in for Addison at work. I don't usually finish until after nine." I run my hands over my pants.

"That's okay. I can wait for you if you want."

I want to immediately say yes, but for some reason, I find myself saying the total opposite. "No, it's okay. I've got tutoring work to get done. My life is so much fun."

"No, it's not. But I am going to make it exciting."

"Yeah, right. You'll be packing up and leaving in the coming months. You've got a big bad world to visit and see." I step out from under his arm.

I wasn't planning on saying that to him. Thinking he's going to leave hurts, and I don't want him to go. I can't bring myself to look up at him. I don't want to see pain in those beautiful brown eyes. "Anyway, I'll catch up with you later. I've got to swing by the library first and then class." I lie about the library. I know I need to separate myself from him before I end up hurt.

Turning to walk away, Aiden says, "Go on a date with me, Elsie?"

I pause mid-step. Slowly, my shoe connects with the hard pavement. "Sorry, what?" I ask, not sure if I've heard him right.

"A date. Friday night. You and me." Aiden gestures between us. He grins that panty-melting smile—one that gets all the girls' blood pumping.

I watch as a group of girls walks by. One of them even has the balls to walk right between us, and my mouth drops open at her rudeness.

Aiden reaches and takes my hand. Then, my focus is back on him, so I glance down at our linked hands. "Come on, firecracker. A date. Let's go out." He gently tugs on my arm.

I chew my lip. "Is this a good idea?"

Aiden's eyes drop, as does my stomach. "We're friends, Elsie. Is it wrong for me to ask a friend to have food and a little fun with me?" He clears his throat, releasing my hand.

"I'll let you know." It's all I can manage right now. "Here, I'll give you my number."

We exchange phone numbers, and Aiden is mostly silent.

I know I've hurt him. It wasn't my intention, but since the chat with Addison this morning, I've found myself second-guessing everything I feel for him.

Yesterday, I wouldn't have hesitated to say yes.

Funny how people can change your thoughts with a simple five-minute chat.

The week flies by. I haven't really spoken to Aiden much, and I still haven't let him know about the date, which should happen tonight.

"What are you doing later?" Addison asks as she takes a drink from the fridge. I stand at the counter of the café on the Friday afternoon shift.

"I'm not sure. Aiden asked me earlier this week to go on a date with him. I still haven't answered him, though."

Addison's eyes go wide. "Why didn't you say yes?"

I fold my arms across my chest and purse my lips, then

say, "Because I had your annoying voice in my head basically telling me I shouldn't fall for him."

Her mouth forms an *O* shape. "I'm sorry. Don't listen to me, Els. I didn't mean for you to second-guess yourself. I just don't want to see you get hurt."

I sigh. "I know, and you're right. I do fall hard and fast. I've already kind of fallen for him, and I don't want those feelings to develop any more than what they already have, because I don't want to end up hurt."

Addison steps around the counter and wraps me in her arms. Stepping back, she says, "Go on the damn date, girl. Have fun, and if you need a shoulder to cry on, I'll be here. What I said the other day was more a small warning, in a way. We've only known him two weeks, and I don't want you hurt. I guess getting hurt by boys is a part of life, though. We all have to experience the hard parts of dating, and that includes the break-up." She shrugs.

"So, I should go?"

Addison nods, smiling.

"Okay. I'll message him."

As I finish, the door opens, and both Addison's and my heads turn.

Aiden's standing there. *Speak of the devil.*

The grin on her face tells me she possibly had something to do with it. I turn back to Addison, smile, and shake my head. "Did you plan this?" I whisper.

"He told me what had happened. So, I was waiting until now to talk to you about it. Go… have fun, Elsie."

I glance at my watch. It's five in the afternoon. "But I'm not finished yet."

"Yes, you are. I'm going to cover you for the last hour before shift change."

My lips pull into a smile. "Are you sure?"

"Yes," she almost shouts.

"Come on, firecracker. I've got something fun planned."

I bet he does—fun is Aiden's middle name.

"It better not be anything stupid or way out there, like jumping off a cliff. Also, you're not allowed to dare me to do anything tonight." Not that I'd refuse another kiss, but who the hell knows what else he'll have me do.

Aiden holds his hand up as if he's swearing on a bible in front of a judge while his other is placed over his chest. "I promise you'll have fun, and that's the only dare I'll give you. I dare you to have fun."

I roll my eyes and turn to Addison, who's got a stupid grin on her face.

"Get out of here before I have to literally kick you in the bum," Addison says.

"Okay, okay. Let me get my stuff." I rush out to the office and grab my bag. When I come back out front, I catch Addison giving Aiden a serious look. Obviously, I've missed something. I don't have time to think on it before Addison walks to the door, pulls it open, and waves her arm in an attempt to get us out quicker.

"Let's get outta here before she loses her biscuits."

Aiden laughs, taking my hand and leading me outside.

"Bye," I say as I'm being dragged out the door.

Addison gives me a little wave.

Aiden leads me to Parker's car. I pause. "Please tell me he knows you have his car."

He chuckles. "Of course. I'm not a thief. Hop in." Aiden pulls the passenger door open, and I climb in, as does he, and releases a sigh. "All right. Take this." He hands me a penny.

Now, I am officially confused.

"Is this what I get to spend on our date?" I cock an eyebrow.

He laughs and starts the car. "Nope, you're in charge of where we end up."

"That makes no sense." I study the coin in my hand before I glance over at him.

"The plan is… we pick a number. Then, we're going to take a coin and flip it at every corner and intersection to the number we pick, and that will lead us to wherever we end up. That's where we have our date."

"This is new. I've never done this before. What if we end up at a dumpster behind a dodgy building?" I laugh.

"That's why I'm leaving you in charge. That way, I can blame you for wherever we end up."

I reach over and shove his shoulder. "Well, let's hope it turns out to be somewhere great."

"All right, now heads is left and tails is right. Pick a number."

My automatic response is, "Five."

"Five?" he asks.

I nod.

Aiden starts driving, and we head to the end of the street—our first intersection.

"What if there's a straight option?" I gesture to the road across the intersection.

He shakes his head. "Nope, left or right, unless there's not one or the other."

"Okay." I grip the coin, ready for use.

"Time to flip before I get another car up my butt."

I flick the coin up and catch it and then flip it over onto the back of my hand.

"Heads." Aiden turns on the indicator, and when the road is clear, he turns left. I know this road, and there's quite a bit of straight. The joys of living in a smallish town.

"No cheating, either. I'm trusting you to let this be a surprise."

"I promise I won't cheat unless it's needed." I laugh. I turn to look at him—he has the biggest smile on his face. He always does. The only time I've seen him unhappy is when he spoke about his friend Tom. It wasn't hard to miss his solemn expression in that moment. I rather the happy-go-lucky Aiden any day. He has a way of making you feel good—although I do like the kissing too, of course. That's an added bonus. The energy he pushes out into the world is what people relish to be around. He can make people laugh and boost them up. Perhaps that's why I'm drawn to him.

"Time to stop staring at me and flip." His voice pulls me from my thoughts. My cheeks warm as I realize I was caught drinking him in like a cold drink of water on a hot day.

Shaking my head, I flip the coin. "Heads." Left again. "Are you prepared if we end up at an empty field?" I glance over at him and then back at the windscreen. My palms have become sweaty. I put the coin in the drink holder and then rub them up and down my jeans. *Why does he make me so nervous?* My heart always races when it comes to Aiden. Even the mention of him gets it going as if I've just gone on a run. It's crazy.

His eyebrows bounce up and down, and I laugh.

"I'm prepared for anything and everything. You have no idea," he says.

"Cocky much?" I reply dryly.

"Oh, firecracker, you like to push the flirting buttons, don't ya?"

I scoff. "Flirting buttons? What even is that? You're the one who pushes them… whatever they are." I pick the coin up as we near another intersection. I flip it and reveal it as we get close. "Before you push another button, it's tails, right?"

He nods. "What's been with your silence this week?" he asks.

I bite my bottom lip, wondering if I should tell him the truth or not. "I was unsure if this…"—I gesture between us—"should happen."

Aiden turns to me, his brow furrowed. "Why?"

I attempt to clear the nervousness from my throat. "Because you've only just come out of a relationship, and I'd rather not be the rebound girl."

Aiden reaches over and takes my hand. "Trust me, you're not a rebound girl. You're *the girl* who makes my heart race. The one who's a firecracker and who pushes those flirty buttons." He chuckles. "We don't have to rush into anything. Let's enjoy each other's company and maybe a few kisses." He shrugs, and again, he has me smiling with all the uncertainty wiped away. Though, for some reason, I can't shake the feeling that there's something he's not telling me.

I pause for a moment before I respond, "Okay. Next time I go radio silent, just show up at my dorm door."

"Don't worry. I will."

I look over, and he winks.

My stomach somersaults.

CHAPTER
Seventeen

Aiden

ell her! My subconscious screams.

If it were a person, I think it would wring my neck for my stupidity. *Why can't I tell her the truth?* Perhaps it's better if I say nothing, but then, Parker is sure to say something, so I bite the bullet. "Look I should tell you that my girlfriend and I were never really together." I swallow another lie, even if it is a micro one. I keep piling them one on the other.

"What? Like never really a couple?"

I nod. "Yeah, we were friends with benefits." I catch her hand entwining ours together, and the smile is wiped from her face.

"So, like… what is kind of happening here." Her finger moves between us.

Damn, wrong choice of words.

I shouldn't have said anything.

I reach over and take her hand. "No, nothing like this. She was a convenience thing… that's what it was to both of us. She knew I was coming here, and yeah, so we just never agreed it was an actual relationship, although we were exclusive to each other. What me and you have…" I pause for a moment to gather my next words carefully before I ruin this and she never talks to me again. "It's more than what I had before. So much more. You set my heart on fire, and I sound super corny saying it like that, but it's the truth. From the moment I met you in that library, I knew I wanted to get to know you." I wish I wasn't pouring out my heart when we are driving, because I want to pull over, take her face in my hands, and kiss those perfect plump lips.

"You're not just saying this to get in my pants?"

"I wouldn't do that, even though getting into them might be a challenge in itself. I don't think they'd fit me."

Elsie throws herself forward, laughing so hard that, a moment later, I catch tears glistening on her cheeks. "You completely took the expression 'get in my pants' and turned it into something totally different. You're something else, Aiden. I never know what to expect with you."

I give her a side glance.

We continue to flip the coin for the remaining two turns, and then I pull up after our last flip.

We're in the city.

When I look out my window, we've ended up in front of an ax-throwing place.

"Well, well, well… looks like we get to throw sharp objects tonight." I wink.

Elsie follows my gaze. I'm not sure if she's happy or sad. Only moments ago, she was smiling and laughing. Now, she's gone silent.

I reach over and take her hand. She turns toward me with a weak smile on her face. "To be honest, I'm a little scared about throwing axes."

I squeeze her hand. "It'll be fine. I'm sure they have safety in place. Take a chance, Elsie. Then, we can grab a bite to eat and maybe go down to the beach."

"All right, I'll give it a go."

I sigh, thankful that she's giving it a try.

We climb out of the car and head inside. The night has a slight chill to it, and the town is alive with the weekend hustle.

"Is there something going on? This city is busier than usual."

Elsie takes a moment and looks around at the people walking by. She glances down at her phone, then I see it; there's a small smile on her face. "It's the Morning Walkers Festival."

"What's that?" I haven't seen anything about a festival.

"It's when a heap of people gather on the beach all night. There are markets and stuff, but the highlight of the festival is when the sun starts to rise the following morning. Everyone runs into the ocean and swims as the sun rises over the horizon. It's like a big party, and it feels kind of spiritual in a way, because you're basking in the early morning sun… kind of like starting fresh."

This sounds interesting and fun. "Wow! I've never heard about it. Do you want to do it tonight?"

She cocks an eyebrow.

I hold my hands out. "Only if you want to. No pressure."

"I'm not so sure."

"You do realize that you need to live a little. Come on, firecracker, do it with me? I've not done anything like this before."

She rolls her eyes and finally nods.

I pull her into my arms and hug her. "Thanks."

She smells like a breath of fresh air. Something I've been needing so badly. The death of Tom was hard for me. When he passed away, his spirit must have decided to take a piece of me with it, because I felt so empty. The kind of empty where you have no idea what you want to do with your life. The kind of empty where you wander aimlessly through the days, not really having any purpose.

"Let's go throw sharp things and not injure ourselves," she says against my chest.

I have no idea why I came here. Well, the college was the only place that would take me so late, but it seems like it was meant to be. This place and the people have lifted the heaviness I've had resting on my chest for over twelve months now.

Stepping inside, it smells like wood, and I hear the thud of axes hitting boards. There are quite a few people here tonight. I buy us one round each, and the workers set us up and give us all guidelines to keep us safe. There's mesh between each person's stall—I guess to make sure no one throws too crazily.

"You wanna go first?" I ask Elsie as she takes a seat, her eyes wide and darting around the rather large room.

"Have you done this before?" She faces me.

"No. It looks like it's going to be fun, though. I think you should go first; that way I can learn from your mistakes."

Her lips pull up on one side. I don't think it would bother me so long as she gave me mouth to mouth and revived me when I passed out because she took my breath away.

"I think you should go. I'd rather watch how you do it."

I get up and take my first ax. There's a target board at the end of the wide—yet kind of short—barricade. I give Elsie a wink and take up my position behind the line on the ground.

Don't make a fool of yourself, Aiden.

"Whoop, whoop, go big boy!"

I turn to Elsie, who's pissing herself laughing; her arms are hugging her stomach so tightly.

"Stop distracting me, woman."

"I'm not a woman. I'm a queen."

I turn to face her and bow. "My apologies, Queen Firecracker."

"Oh, shut it and take your turn or I'll throw one at you," she teases.

Facing the target again, I follow the instructions the worker gave us. I release the ax at the right time, and a loud thud follows, but I watch, horrified, as my ax simply bounces off the wall.

I don't hear anything behind me, but upon turning around, Elsie's sitting there, red in the face, trying not to laugh. She holds her hands out, giving me a thumbs up. "Good job," is all she manages before I lose her to fits of laughter.

"Come on then. You wanna piss yourself laughing at me? It's my turn to make fun of you."

She mumbles something under her breath.

"What was that?"

"Oh nothing," she replies with such an innocence to her voice. I automatically know she's up to no good.

"Is this how you do it?" She stands the same way I was, and her arm pulls back, and then she moves so quick that I miss it when she lets it go. Her ax smacks right in the center of the target.

I leap out of my chair. "You've done this before!" I shout, not caring about the other people around us.

She points toward a wall. I follow her line of sight to a wall of photographs. I walk over there and scan the images until I focus in on one. A familiar face stares right back to me. In the image, she rests an ax on one shoulder, and on the other, she has a champion's belt.

"My secret hobby." Her warm breath hits my ear while electricity shoots down my spine.

I whip around. "You totally played me, didn't ya?"

She shrugs. "The coin got us here. I promise I didn't lie about those, but yeah…I had you going from the beginning, and the guys here know me. They know that if I bring people, to not say anything."

I step closer to her. My arms wrap around her waist, and I lean down until our faces are inches apart. "Now that's hot," I whisper before pulling her tightly against me and pressing my lips to hers. Everything comes alive between us. Our breathing becomes heavy, and her tongue glides against mine. I want to take her out of here and discover her body in a way that will have her never wanting another guy.

Elsie places one last kiss against my lips before taking a small step back. "Wow. Take my breath away, why don't you," she says, her cheeks flushed red.

"That's my plan."

"What?"

"To make you lose your breath every time I kiss or touch you." I reach out and take her hand and rub her knuckles.

"If you keep doing that, you'll make me pass out."

"Haha… you're a joker, aren't ya?" I don't give her a chance to respond before I pull her against me again. The heat from her body against mine is what I want every day. It's what I seem to be missing in my life. Back home, I was known as the playboy, and boy, did I live up to that name. There comes a time when you have to change—or at least try to make a change. Coming here was that decision for me. I didn't plan on falling for the girl in my arms, but I have.

"You love it," she teases. Her head lifts off my chest, and she stares up at me. That puppy-dog type of stare holds me completely hostage.

"I'll put up with it." I waggle my eyebrows.

Elsie shoves me in the chest, pushing herself off me. "You're a pain in the butt. Let's finish what we paid for. I'm getting hungry, and you don't want to mess with me when you meet the other side of me… the hangry side. She can be a real bitch." Her finger points into my chest, then she walks back to where we were playing.

I pay close attention to how her body moves. The way her hips shift in those pants twists my stomach in a good way.

CHAPTER
Eighteen

Elsie

An hour later and another round of axes, we're walking out, and I've totally wiped the floor with his ego.

His hip bumps mine. "You know, you could have warned me I didn't stand a chance."

"Where would the fun be in that?" I glance over at him. "Don't worry, not many people can beat me. No one realizes how much I come here."

"So, you enter in competitions?" We walk side by side, my hand itching to take his. I crave his closeness.

As if he reads my thoughts, his arm drops over my shoulder then slides down to my waist. Instinctively, I do the same. Here we are, walking down the street like a couple.

We stop in at The Salad Bar. It's the one place I love going. The food they sell here is divine.

"You a bit of a health nut?"

I stop perusing the menu, even though I already know what I'm going to get. "I wouldn't say health nut, or whatever that is. I've got my own personal stash of sweets and candy back in my room. But I do love this place. Their food is always so delicious. You haven't lived unless you've tried their whole menu." I wave my hand over the paper in front of me.

Aiden gives me a funny look, his eyes shifting between myself and the menu. "You've eaten everything they make here?"

I shrug. "Yeah. What's wrong with that?"

"I didn't say there was anything wrong with it. I've never known anyone to have eaten everything off one menu in a restaurant before."

"What can I say? I lead an exciting life."

The waitress is back. She smiles down at me. "You ready to order?" Her focus turns to Aiden. "Are you ready to order?"

Aiden's head pops up, and he finally realizes what's going on. "Do you know what you're getting? I didn't hear you order."

"Yep, I'm getting the pumpkin and feta salad. It's my favorite, and they know that here." I smile up at the waitress.

"Okay then, I'll trust you. I'll have the same, please."

She takes the menus away. It's a quaint little restaurant with candles on every table. They are only lit when people sit at them, so it has a romantic feel. Dark wood walls with photo frames covering them. There are images of the town back in the olden days, as people tend to call it. This building has been around since the town was first built, and the owners restored and turned it into the restaurant. I love history—I guess that's why I'm so drawn to this place.

A silence falls over the table.

"Have you had fun tonight?" Aiden asks.

"Yeah, totally. No one has ever taken me on a date like this—or gone to this much effort, I should say."

"Why not? I'm sure you've dated plenty of guys. Well, I just assume you would have."

I scoff. "Oh, I've had dates, but let's just say a couple of the guys were only interested in one thing. Oh well, story of my life." I chew on the side of my mouth.

Aiden's jaw muscle tenses then releases. "One day, it'll change."

I roll my eyes. "Yeah, whatever. I'm only good for a short time. Like when you leave. This is just a vacation thing." My hand waves between us, and the hurt which stabs me in the chest is not something I've experienced with any other guy. For some reason, I knew my old boyfriends were short-term, but with Aiden, I really do wish it could be more than a simple fling. Who knows what the future holds?

"Can we not discuss what's happening between us and comparing it to other guys who have come and gone in your life?" Tension drips from Aiden's words.

"It's the truth, though." I half-laugh, trying to make light of the conversation. "You are going to leave eventually, and this will be nothing but a fling to you. I may not accept it right now, and it's the reason I've been attempting to keep my distance, but you also had a girlfriend, which is another reason to back away." I take a breath. My focus is now firmly on Aiden. "The way I see it, I'm the one who will walk away from this carrying a broken heart. You're the carefree playboy, and I'm the girl who was a part of your life for a short while." I hold myself together. I don't want my emotions to get the better of me, allowing him to see how much he already affects me.

Aiden reaches across the table and takes my hand. A small, very small part of me wants to pull back. I can't, though. He's stamped his presence on my heart, and now I have to learn how to cope with whatever happens between us.

"Elsie, let's live in the now and see where it goes. I like you."

I take a moment to let his words sink in. *He likes me. Actually, likes me.*

I open my mouth to respond, but we're interrupted by our dinner arriving. My mouth waters as I stare down at my plate. Nothing more is said about the future of our relationship. It's probably for the best. I'll simply have to wait and see what happens.

After a silent meal and a quiet walk down to the beach, I suddenly don't feel like hanging around for sunrise, let alone swimming in the water.

There are a number of people on the beach, and stalls are being set up. We aimlessly stroll around and stop at shops. I stop at one stall who is selling jewelry. There's a silver ring with a plain band, but it has a pink stone which, going by the price, is a cubic zirconia. It's cute, quaint, and perfectly me. I want it. I reach into my bag to retrieve my wallet when a hand touches my elbow.

"I'll get that for ya." He's already got money out and is handing it over to the chick standing in front of us.

"Oh, you don't have to do that."

Receiving his change, he turns to me. "I know that, but I want to."

I grin. "Thank you. Isn't it perfect?" I slip it onto my

slender finger and hold my hand out in front of me, waving the ring around.

Aiden's hand takes mine. "Yes, it's perfect." His voice is sultry. He leans over and presses his lips to my cheek, and with that one sweet motion, my stomach twists and butterflies tickle my insides.

"You're a smooth man, Aiden." I chuckle, reaching up and tucking a couple of strands of hair behind my ear then glancing up at him through my eyelashes.

"You're worth every bit of smoothness, Elsie."

I roll my eyes, and a smirk pulls across my face. "I want to get something sweet. Let's go over to that churro stand. It's calling my name."

He doesn't release my hand. Instead, he entwines our fingers together and leads me to that place I want to go.

We spend the next couple of hours walking the beach.

I've slipped my shoes off so I don't get the annoying sand stuck between my toes. There's a tug-of-war going on inside me. I sense a storm brewing, and I don't know why. Tonight has been perfect, and Aiden is flawless in every way. So, why can't I shake the uneasy feeling taking up camp in my stomach?

"You all right?" Aiden squeezes my hand, and I'm pulled back from my thoughts.

I lift my arm to look at my watch. It's almost midnight. I yawn at the thought of even attempting to get out of bed in the morning. "I'm feeling pretty tired. I'm not sure I'll function for work tomorrow."

I know I have the afternoon shift and can sleep in, but I'm worried about falling for this Aussie guy standing next to me. I need to guard myself, even though everything inside of me is screaming to let down the barriers I've put up.

"We can go if you want. It's all good." He pulls me against him, and our bodies mesh together perfectly.

"I think that would be good. I've had a great night, Aiden." I pull out from under his arm and step in front of him. "This is what I've needed, and I'm enjoying getting to know you. You're awesome. Thanks for my ring… I love it." Holding my hand in front of me, I turn and flash the fake gem at Aiden. He grins, stepping closer. His protective arms slip around my waist, and I'm flush against him, staring up at those shimmering blue eyes.

No words are needed.

No questions are asked.

His mouth touches mine.

My eyes flutter shut while waves of euphoria float through me. Our tongues explore each other's mouths. His arms tighten while he holds me against him. My hands cup his face as heat prickles my skin. I want more from him. To explore those abs under his shirt.

Aiden pulls back, and I'm left breathless. "Let's get you home before I take advantage of you right here on the beach."

I smirk, batting my eyelashes. "Now, now, that won't be happening, especially on a beach. I'm not prepared to have sand in places where it shouldn't be. It wouldn't be pretty. And I'm sure your appendage wouldn't like to have something similar to sandpaper rubbing in places you don't want it to."

His face screws up as he thinks about what I've said. "Yeah, don't go into details. I die in the pants just thinking about somethin' like that happenin.'"

I laugh at his thick Australian accent, but every time he speaks, it's another reminder that he's only here for a short time.

CHAPTER
Nineteen

Aiden

After parking the car back at the house, I walk Elsie to her dorm room then head home again. We'd decided not to do the jump tomorrow—Elsie isn't ready.

Stepping onto the street, the night is silent. It's peaceful. It forces me to think about things and what I want. *Can I leave now, knowing how I feel about Elsie?* She's been hot and cold since the beginning, and I'm thinking it's because of me. She's not a vacation fling. She's so much more, and I wish she could see that. I need her to see that. I don't know how to get her to understand.

I slip my key into the door and silently step inside. I'm met with darkness aside from a light on in the pantry. I slide my shoes off and walk to the kitchen to grab a bottle of water from the fridge. After pulling the door open, I grab one, then shut it, then I jump back at the person standing behind the door.

"What the hell?" I grab my chest. My heart nearly took a leap out of my throat. "Don't sneak up on people like that. Were you waiting for me?"

I cock an eyebrow at Addison who's standing there in one of Parker's shirts and short shorts.

The grin on her face tells me what I need to know. "I might have been. Though, honestly, I'd rather be sleeping. But I wanted to talk to you without the others around." She slides onto the stool.

I lean against the bench and wait to hear what she has to say. She's Elsie's best friend, so it could be any number of things. Then it dawns on me. *Did Parker tell her my secret?* He said he wouldn't.

"I'm all ears," I say, twisting the cap off the water bottle.

There's silence. I watch her play with crumbs on the bench, her head's low, then her eyes meet mine. "I'm going to tell you this once. So, consider this your warning…" She pauses. I nod. "Do *not* hurt my friend."

"I wasn't planning to," I cut in before she continues.

She gives me a deadpan look meaning, *"Shut the hell up and let me finish."* I press my lips together, forming a thin line.

"She won't admit this, but she's fragile. Every boy she's gotten close to has only wanted her for one thing. She has a kind heart and takes every heartache like a champion. When it comes to you, I'm not sure if she'll recover as quickly. She's very guarded, and you've both only known each other a short while. If you intend to use her like the others, then I suggest you walk away. Now."

I hold my hands up. "Whoa, stop right there. I'm not one

of those guys. I'm not a douchebag who only uses girls for *one thing*. That's not who I am. Maybe it's who I once was, but not anymore." My chest tightens, and I'm becoming angry. I know she's looking out for her friend, but damn.

"All I'm saying is to really think about where you stand with her. I know she really likes you. I don't want to see her get hurt. You're going to be leaving in a couple of months. Then what?" She raises her hands, shrugging.

"Honestly, I don't know. I really like her as well, and I've told her so. She's been up and down about the whole thing." My head drops and looks at the water bottle that I'm now shredding the label on.

"She's being guarded because I've told her not to fall for you."

My head whips up. "What?" I almost growl.

"I want her guarded so she can make a good decision that won't get her hurt in the end. I've not had a chance to talk to the other guys she's dated, but you're here, and you're Parker's friend, so I think I have every right to step in the middle of this, or it'll put a strain on our friendships. Parker is always looking out for her, like he does his sister."

"I can see where you're coming from." I already knew that it was possible I was going to hurt Elsie. I'm a terrible person. *My stupid lie.* It's like a punch-to-the-gut reminder of how stupid I was in setting that whole thing up.

Addison rises from the stool. "Remember what I said, and if you intend to take your relationship to the status of boyfriend and girlfriend, then make sure everything is laid out on the table. No skeletons in the closet. Elsie is an open book. She will tell you how it is. Also, tell her that no matter the distance, she'll mean everything to you if that's how you feel."

"She already does." I swallow.

Addison's hand drops on my shoulder. "I'm glad we could have this chat. Now, once again… don't hurt my friend. She'll probably murder you if you do, so I'm more so protecting you than her, in all honesty." She chuckles.

After witnessing Elsie's ax-throwing skills earlier, I think I'd probably be castrated if I didn't treat her right.

Addison walks out, and I'm left standing there wondering about my next move.

I need to tell Elsie about the lie.

On Sunday, a couple of days after my perfect date with Elsie and the firm talking-to from Addison, I sit on the couch with my laptop open. Pulling up my emails since I've been so busy with practice, I haven't had a chance to check them. When they pop up, I notice a reply from Elsie saying she'd love to help me. I hit reply.

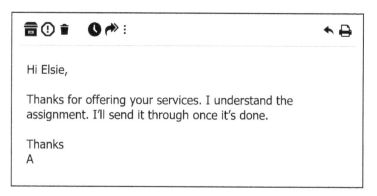

Hi Elsie,

Thanks for offering your services. I understand the assignment. I'll send it through once it's done.

Thanks
A

As I hit send, the door flies open, and a rush of voices flow through, and my heart speeds up at the sound of one particular person. *Elsie.*

"Get ready, Aiden. We're heading to the beach today," Parker announces as he walks through and goes straight to his room. Addison heads to the kitchen already dressed in her beachwear. I wait, and that's when I spot her. Elsie steps around the corner ever so slowly with a beaming smile on her face. My lips pull up instantly because she has that kind of effect on me.

"Hey," she greets. Elsie stands there in a short sky-blue dress, and I itch to touch her and press my lips to hers. The urgency overtakes me.

"Hey there." I stand with my laptop. I take her hand in mine and lead her down to my room so I can grab what I need, but also so I can taste her again.

She walks with me.

I hear her giggle as we step into my room, and I kick my door shut then push her against it. "I've missed these lips," I say through a passionate kiss.

"Is that all you've missed?" I hear her teasing tone.

I pull back. "Of course not. These lips are connected to the perfect girl. She's who I truly miss."

Elsie's mouth turns up on one side, and her cheeks go pink. "You're a smooth talker, Aussie guy." She nods as if agreeing with herself, and it's so cute. "The only thing you need to learn is to keep in contact with the person you actually have feelings for."

My brow knits together. "I'm sorry?"

Her hand touches my face. "When you see me, make sure to tell me how you feel, and you're happy to kiss these lips you've missed so much, but what about a random message now and again to see how my day is going? You do have my number."

Damn it. "I seriously suck at the text messaging thing. I know every teenager loves their phone, but I'm one of those who rarely checks it or posts on their social media." I pause and pull her against my chest. Her shining eyes beam up at me. "I will try harder. Promise." And then I seal the promise with another kiss.

"You better get ready, or your door is going to get knocked down by one of the guys." I reluctantly release my hold on her, knowing she's right.

"If you say so. Off ya go so I can get changed—unless you wanna get a sneak peek." I waggle my eyebrows teasingly. I watch as she bites her bottom lip then turns and walks out.

Damn.

CHAPTER
Twenty

Elsie

It was so tempting to stay. I'm not that girl, though, even if the guy is offering. I've learned my lesson to make them work for all the girly goods I have to offer. It's not going to change with the Australian guy, even if he has a heart-stopping accent and perfect lips.

Walking down the hall, staring at my feet, I can't wipe this stupid smile from my face.

"What are you doing, little miss?"

My head flicks up when I jump, noticing Addison standing in Parker's bedroom doorway.

"Damn, you scared the life out of me." My hand rests over my startled heart.

"You were too busy dreaming about Mr. Aussie Guy in the next room. Don't think I missed him snatching you out of the room the moment we walked through the door."

"He missed me." I shrug.

"Yeah, I bet he did."

"Shut up." I push her shoulder, and we laugh.

We pile out of the cars when we arrive at the beach. Dane, Paislee, and Jimmy all came together, and Parker, Addison, Aiden, and I all went in Parker's car. It's a beautiful day for the beach—the sun is hot, the sand is warm, and the water is sure to be refreshing.

I slip off my flip-flops and pull my short, blue dress over my head to go straight for the water. There's no way I'd get in if it was freezing. I'm in a black one-piece—totally not a bikini girl. I get the sense that I'm being watched, so I stop when I see Aiden, who looks like a fool as he stares in my direction.

"Shut your mouth. You're drooling," Jimmy shouts at Aiden, who quickly snaps out of his trance and shoves Jimmy in the shoulder as he walks past him.

"Oh, hell, he's got the hots for you." Paislee slips in beside me in a bright-pink bikini. She looks stunning. I search for Dane, and he's doing the exact same thing with Paislee as Aiden was with me a moment ago.

"You're a little late to the party. We've been going on dates and actually kissing." I drop my dress and reach for the lotion, squirt a little into my hand, and rub it up my arms and over my face.

"Are you serious? That's so exciting." Paislee pulls me in for a weird hug I clearly wasn't ready for.

"Yeah, it's exciting but also worrisome because he's going to leave soon." I shrug and start walking toward the water which glides against the sandy shore. So peaceful.

"Girl, just enjoy the time you have together. It's not every day you get to have a fling with someone as gorgeous as him."

"That's the thing…" I sigh. "I'm not so sure I want to be the *holiday fling*."

Squealing behind us causes us to turn. Parker has hauled Addison over his shoulder and is running toward us. We both chuckle as they crash into the water in the most ungraceful way.

"Then don't go there with him," Paislee says.

My smile drops. "That's the other thing… I don't think I can keep away. Every time I pull back, he's right there in front of me again. How am I supposed to walk away from that?" I raise my eyebrow as a body runs past us.

Paislee sucks in a breath. "Well, damn. Yeah, not sure how you're going to survive a body like that."

"It's not just about the body. He makes me laugh." My eyes haven't left Aiden as he stands in the water then walks out deeper. His tanned body is lickable. Then, he swims back to us, and my breath leaves me. I know I've already seen him with his shirt off, but he's wet now, and all those droplets are running down his gorgeous skin. Yep, all my fantasies have come true at once.

"Shut your mouth."

I hadn't realized it was open, so I quickly snap it shut.

"Just go enjoy him. Don't make any decision right now." Paislee's words are a slap back to reality. I do need to enjoy myself, and I have been. Only there is this cloud hanging over me—an uncertainty that makes it hard for me to fully commit myself to Aiden.

Just enjoy him.

Paislee takes off into the ocean. I stand in ankle-deep water, simply staring out over the deep-blue ocean. Imagine all the secrets it's washed away. So many people come to the beach for peace. They whisper their problems, and the words wash out, leaving you with serenity.

Large arms wrap around my waist. I startle and squeal playfully as I'm being carried into the deeper water.

"Time to get wet and stop teasing me," Aiden's deep voice whispers in my ear. Goose bumps prickle immediately all over my whole body. When the water gets to waist high, he falls, and we both go down and under the water. His grip loosens when I stand up. I turn, and Aiden's head pops out of the water. He flicks his hair, and it somehow manages to fall into place.

Aiden's hands grip my swimsuit, and he pulls me against him. My legs have a mind of their own and wrap around his waist.

Paislee's words ring in my mind again. *Just enjoy him.*

So that's what I'm going to do. When the time comes for him to leave, we can make a decision about where we stand, even though I know deep down I'll walk away with a broken heart.

But what's life without a little heartbreak?

"You're teasing me in these togs."

I screw my face up at the unfamiliar name. "What are you talking about?"

Aiden laughs then pulls me in for a kiss. I want to pull back because we're in front of everyone, but I don't.

"What do you call them?" He tugs at the strap of my swimmers giving me a hint.

"Ah… it's called a swimsuit. What even is the word *togs?*"

Our bodies move together with the waves of the ocean. My arms wrap around his neck while feeling his smooth skin against mine, which is so smooth to the touch.

"They're togs… you know… swimwear." He shrugs.

"You just sound like you're making words up now," I tease.

"Come off it. I call them togs. Do you know what a cyclone is?" His question causes another puzzled look. When I don't answer, he tells me, "You call them hurricanes." My mouth forms an *O* as I register the familiarity.

"It just sounds weird. I mean, we all speak English, but the way you speak is very…" I pause, looking for the right word.

"Bogan," he ends the sentence.

"What is a bogan?" I can't help the laughter the word causes.

"Very Australian. Some of us refer to ourselves that way because we're so laid-back."

"Sounds like a silly word."

"I guess you could say I'm from Venus and you're from Mars." He leans in and steals another kiss.

"I guess so, but at least you don't kiss like a fish."

Aiden throws his head back, laughing.

"What's so funny?" Parker asks as he and Addison make their way over to us.

"I'm making fun of Aiden and his weird words. He calls swimsuits togs."

Parker chuckles, and Addison's expression is the same as mine was when he told me.

"Now, that's just weird," Addison says as she swims up to Parker. I make a move, slipping my legs from around Aiden's waist. He grips my leg to stop me and pulls me back against him. I turn to him, and when I stare into his eyes, they shine with a bright light.

"It's not that bad. All right, so your football is Gridiron. Australian football is definitely not how you fellas play. You'll have to watch one of our games to really understand. I say lollies… you call them candy. We say holiday… you say vacation. We simply say, 'I need to use the toilet.' You guys say 'restroom' or 'bathroom'… it's so proper." Aiden holds his nose up in a posh way. I splash water at him, laughing.

"Proper my ass," I say.

We spend the next hour bobbing around in the beautiful water. There's more teasing on Aiden's part and laughter from the both of us.

"All right, it's time for this wrinkled girl to get out," I say.

Addison and Paislee murmur in agreement.

I'm sure Dane and Paislee have been fighting the urge to mount each other. The way they're looking at one another, like they're a pair of hungry wolves who want to devour each other's swimwear, brings a grin to my face.

"What are you smiling about?" Aiden's hand wraps around my waist from behind and pulls me back to him.

Twisting my head, I whisper into his ear, "Paislee and Dane. They're struggling with this 'no touching' business."

Aiden nods. His warm breath hits my ear again, which causes tingles to dance down my spine. "I'd hate to not be able to touch you like this. To feel your body pressed against mine." His lips press on the bare skin of my shoulder. Even though I'm in cool water, my body turns hot with his words and his touch.

I climb off him. "Tame yourself, Aussie guy," I joke and start swimming for the shore. Addison and Paislee are already hitting the shallower water and walking out, so I race to catch up with them.

"Look at you and Aussie guy getting all cozy," Addison coos.

Nothing could wipe the smile from my face. "I'm listening to the wise words of Paislee and '*just enjoying him.*'" I nibble my bottom lip.

"You pair need a room, that's what you need," Paislee shoots my way.

"Look at you, getting all hot and bothered, not being able to touch your man," I say, and Paislee's mouth drops open then forms a thin line.

"Shut up," she grumbles.

Addison laughs. "Why don't you simply talk to Parker and tell him?"

Paislee is already shaking her head before Addison has finished her sentence. "No way. I'm sure it would cause more problems than fix anything. I was there the day Parker told him to not even go there, that I was off-limits. I'd hate to be the cause of a fight between them."

We arrive back at our position on the sand and pick up our beach towels, wrapping them around our wet bodies.

"I still think it's better having it out there so it can be forgiven, and he can move on. That pair couldn't hate each other; they've been friends for a long time," Addison voices her opinion.

"I agree with Addison." I wipe the wetness from my

body and then lay my towel out to lie on. It's time to get some of the sun's rays on my white skin.

"If only it was that easy for me," Paislee says as she lays out her towel beside mine, and Addison does the same on the opposite side of me.

We settle in and lie there, silent for a while. I listen to the waves, and in the distance, I can hear the boys carrying on like typical males.

"They're so young with the way they act sometimes." Addy takes the words right from my mouth.

"You totally said what I was just thinking," I say, and we laugh.

CHAPTER
Twenty One

Elsie

We stay at the beach until late afternoon, and I know that, even though I put lotion on, I'm burned. Stupid lotion is not doing its job, so we decide to leave.

Once we pack up and take the drive, we all arrive back to the boys' place, order some Chinese, and settle in for the rest of the evening.

"Today was great," I say.

Everyone nods and murmurs their agreement as they shove food into their mouths with chopsticks. I need more days like this, where I'm not worried about schoolwork, tutoring, or basically anything education-related. Sometimes the brain needs a holiday.

"Do you know how long you plan to stay here, Aiden?" Paislee asks.

I almost drop my plate.

A brief silence fills the room as we wait for him to answer while I sit beside him on the floor against the couch. Once he finishes his mouthful of food, Aiden replies, and I hold my breath. "I'm not sure. I have a visa for a year, so I guess we'll see how things go and where I'm going to head after this semester is over. I could possibly stay for another term… I think that's what you guys call it. Sorry, I'm not up to date with the way you fellas run your schools and colleges." He laughs, but I didn't miss the hint of hesitation when he spoke. He's worried he'll say the wrong thing.

"So, you'll hang around here for a while?" If Paislee keeps asking these questions, I'm going to have to butt in because I'm afraid that I'm going to hear something I don't want to.

Aiden clears his throat, and I turn to him. He's watching me with a heavy stare, and with that, a weight has fallen on my chest. "I'm not sure. I want to, but there's also a lot I still want to explore…" His words trail off.

I shift my gaze and stare down at my food—funny, my appetite has now completely gone. Tears begin to well in my eyes. I blink profusely, not wanting them to fall, willing them to go away. Not with everyone around. Dammit, this is what I didn't want to happen.

With a mouth full of food and a lump in my throat, which makes it hard to swallow, I'm sure I look like I've just stuffed food in my cheeks for the hell of it.

A long silence fills the room. I stand. "Sorry, just going to grab a drink. If that's okay."

I feel all their eyes on me, and I really hope they can't see the water still sitting in my eyes.

Parker shifts uncomfortably in his seat. "Yeah, sure. Help yourself."

I walk past those intense gazes and into the kitchen. A hush fills the room as I walk away, and I'm sure Paislee is on the receiving end of some comments for bringing up the conversation. After pulling open the fridge, I pull out a can of soda from the shelf, crack it open, and take a large gulp to wash away the plaster that seems to have coated my throat. I shut the fridge and almost drop the can in my hand.

"Addison, what the hell are you doing? You scared me." I take a breath to steady my racing heart.

"Are you all right?" Her voice is barely a whisper. She pulls me into her arms, and I do everything possible not to cry. I keep swallowing my sobs down—I will *not* cry.

I shuffle out of her arms, needing to escape. A knock at the door gives me my chance. I step back as Parker heads to the door. I don't want to look at Addison's concerned face right now. It only makes it sting even more. I can't even bring myself to look over at Aiden, because that hurts way more than it should.

"What's up, people?" Willow's high-pitched voice bellows through the doorway. It seems like forever since I've seen them.

"Hey, bitches, nice of you to invite us to your little getaway," Addison replies dryly.

Willow waves. "Oh, you'll get over it. Plus, I didn't think you'd want to leave your man."

My brow furrows. "What about me? I don't have a man."

I place my soda on the bench and go give them a hug. I'm so thankful for their arrival and distraction from the previous conversation.

Willow and Jane give each other a knowing glance. Then,

Jane responds, "That's not the rumor on the campus." She shrugs, and my head spins.

"Ah… what rumors?" I push.

Willow's head turns to Aiden, who is still sitting silently on the floor. "News is that you guys have been busy locking lips."

"So, does that automatically mean I'm in a relationship?" The words are harsh when I don't mean for them to be.

Willow's mouth hangs open, then she shuts it but gives me a small smile. "Don't worry. Ignore what I just said."

Yeah, right. Annoyance ripples through my veins. Stupid rumors. I can't even hang out and kiss a guy without people assuming I'm in a relationship. Of course, I'd love to be in one with Aiden, but I don't think that's a good idea. It's only asking for trouble, and like he said before, he's going to move on eventually and go to some other place and probably lock lips with other girls, add another notch to his belt.

Clearing my throat, I say, "Sorry, guys, I'm feeling pretty wrecked. I'm going to call it a night. Got stuff to do before tomorrow." I walk past Addison, who narrows her eyes at me. My lips form a thin line. I collect my bag from the doorway and toss it over my shoulder. "I'll catch you all tomorrow."

I walk back in and grab my soda from the bench.

When I turn, Aiden is waiting at the door, and my step falters. "I'll walk you back to your dorm."

"No, it's all right. Thank you, though." I step around him and through the door. I hear the others shout their goodbyes, but I don't wait and see what Aiden does. I need to escape.

"Please don't hate me." Aiden's voice comes from behind me.

My head whips around. "Why would I hate you? I always knew that this wasn't anything special." Emotion catches my throat, and I blink a few times to clear it away.

"Elsie, wait! Please."

I don't stop. I hear a rush of footsteps, and then Aiden is standing in front of me. His pinched eyebrows and the look of pain in his eyes shows me that this hurts him too.

"Aiden, I think it's time to just call this what it is... nothing. Friends with benefits—or whatever term you use. But I need to put an end to this thing between us, because it hurts too much." The lump is back, bigger than ever, and my chest tightens with each word spoken and breath taken.

"Don't do that," he growls. His face goes slightly red under the streetlamp.

"Do what?" I reply with as much frustration as he has.

"Shut me out. Is this what you do with everyone?" His words slam into my chest.

"No. I'm just the girl who's only good for a one-time show." I raise my eyebrows and purse my lips then step around him and pick up my pace. I'm sure the others can probably hear us having this argument on the footpath. "Now, can we stop making a spectacle of ourselves outside your place because, to be quite honest, I don't need more rumors starting about me," I call over my shoulder.

Aiden races up to walk with me as he lets out a groan. He reaches for my hand, and I let him, even though I shouldn't. I want his touch more than anything right now. To know that he would catch me if I fell and put the pieces of my heart back together if he broke it means so much to me.

Nothing more is said as we walk back across campus and to my empty dorm room. I unlock and open the door then pause with my back to Aiden. I sigh. "You can come in if you want."

"I'm sorry if I hurt you with what I said."

I keep my back to him, go for the table, and dump my bag. I sense him behind me. I don't need to look to know that his hard stare is burning a hole in my back.

I sigh and reluctantly turn to face the guy who seems to have a piece of my heart in his hands but is oblivious to it. "It is what it is. I shouldn't expect anything more. We both know you don't plan to stay. It's fine." I try to brush off the emotions that I'm wearing.

Aiden doesn't appear to accept what I'm saying and takes two strides and envelops me in his arms. Mine automatically respond by latching themselves around him and holding on tight. I didn't want to have these feelings. They suck, majorly. I wish I could stuff them in a box and lock them up, because that would solve a lot of problems with people and relationships.

"It's not fine, and you're not fine. I don't want to hurt you." He buries his face into my neck, and I feel the brush of his lips against my skin. It's as if his touch shoots off electric sparks in my chest—something that's never happened before with anyone I've ever been with. Aiden is different in so many ways.

I press myself tighter to his warmth. I need him to hold me like he's never going to let me go, and I don't think I can let him go either.

I sense his mouth moving up my neck. My head falls back, giving him access. Our breaths quicken. Everything becomes warm, and I want to be out of my little dress and wrap myself around him. I want his body against mine so I can breathe in his musky scent.

My hands ache to explore under his shirt. My fingers skim the bottom hem before taking it and pulling it over his head. His hungry gaze holds mine briefly while he traces the back of his hand over my cheek. My eyes close and drink up his touch like it's a drug I desperately need. A slight moan escapes my lips, and then, seconds later, his mouth finds mine. Aiden moves then pushes me against the door. Our tongues dance and fight to claim each other's mouths.

I glide my fingertips up his smooth chest and reach around his back to pull him closer. My nails bite into his flesh. A moan escapes me in the middle of our wet kisses.

Aiden's hands move to the hem of my blue dress, and he pulls it up over my head. I'm still wearing my swimsuit underneath.

This could get interesting.

He tosses the small piece of material aside and stands before me, his stare claiming every part of my body, and I am just as hungry for him.

"Are you going to stand there and stare?" Words breathlessly rush out from my truly kissed lips. They're swollen from his wild, passionate kisses.

"You're so beautiful." His words are barely a whisper.

My heart leaps with the longing in his gaze as he steps closer to me. Our bodies are an inch apart, but he stands there, not moving. My eyes flutter closed, and my breathing is ragged. So is his. Still, he stands there.

"I want you so bad, but I don't want to hurt you."

The room around me shifts as the reality of our situation rushes back in my mind. I don't want this moment to end. I want his lips all over my sun-kissed skin. I want this moment in case it will never happen again.

Taking charge, my hands go behind his neck, and I pull his mouth to mine. I'm going to take what I can while he's still here. My heart longs for him, and if we decide to make this work, then that's what I'll do—make it work.

I pull back from our tongue dance and stare into his familiar ocean-blue eyes. "Aiden, I'm in this until you say you no longer want anything to do with me. We can remain friends or try something more. The ball is in your court."

He doesn't even wait ten seconds before his mouth rushes to mine again. He lifts me up and holds me against him, then my back is against the door once again with so much lust or love—I'm not sure which—locking us together. His mouth drops from mine and moves down to my neckline.

The strap on one side of my swimsuit is pulled down, exposing more of my upper chest; my breasts are still covered. I feel his lips pick up where they left off and move down until they get to the top of my sensitive breast, which swells and aches for his touch.

"Bedroom…" I breathe.

"Which one?" he breathes out somehow, because his kisses don't stop.

My lower abdomen twists with aches and desire for him. "Across the room."

With ease, he pushes off the door, not bothering to put me down. Aiden carries me as though my weight is nothing for him. He moves quickly and kicks the half-open door wider. My lips attach themselves to his tanned skin around his neck, working their way around the other side, and going back up. I pause halfway and suck.

"Oh my… Elsie," he moans. With one swift move, he's kicked the door shut. "Which bed?"

"Left," I hiss between my teeth. I go back to the same spot and suck again. I desperately want to mark him, to let everyone know we're together.

I don't want anyone else to have him.

He. Is. Mine.

Aiden moves swiftly and gently lays me on the bed. "Are you sure you want to do this?" His large frame hovers over mine.

No words need to be spoken. I smile like a girl who's about to receive a gift she's been dying to get her entire life. I reach behind his neck and pull him back to my lips, giving him the answer he's craving.

CHAPTER
Twenty Two

Elsie

Noise behind the door startles me awake. My bed is empty, with no Aiden to be seen anywhere in the bedroom. My stomach flips anxiously. After a perfect night of exploring each other in ways only lovers can, he's up and left.

I sit up on the bed and glance around for a note, checking the bedside table and the floor to make sure I didn't knock it off.

There is nothing.

I hear Willow and Addison chatting in the other room. With my beaten heart barely beating, I slide my legs over the side of the bed. My elbows are on my knees, and my head falls into my hands. *How could I have been so stupid?* Aiden said all the right words, touched me in all the right places, and ate up my kisses and moans as though they were candy. Obviously, I was something that simply dissolved once the tasty treat was devoured.

Vigorously, I rub my face with my open hands, removing the sleep from the corners of my eyes. I don't even remember what time it was when we fell asleep. Well, I thought he went to sleep, but it seems he waited for me to fall asleep and then left with his tail between his legs after getting what he wanted.

I stand and go to my closet to pull out clothes for the day—a short, light-blue denim skirt and a purple tank top. I need a shower to wash away any remnants of the night before. Grabbing fresh underwear and my clothes, I head out toward the giggling voices.

Addison and Willow turn my way when the door opens. My face must give away how I'm feeling because Addison rushes to me, her forehead pinched together with concern. "What's wrong?"

A lump forms in my throat. I don't want to cry. I won't. Swallowing the lump down even for a few seconds allows me to get out what I need to. "He's gone. He got what he wanted and left." I shut my eyes tight in the hopes that it's just a dream. That he didn't actually leave. And that I'm still asleep. *That's it. It has to be.*

I remember how he spoke to me, how he claimed my body like he would never need anyone else again. His sweet whispers of affection and want made my stomach drop. *He really left.*

Addison takes me in her arms, but I've become numb. Having no feelings would be better than the pain I'm feeling right now. "Elsie, I don't think he left to get away. Aiden wasn't even at the house this morning when the boys were up getting ready for practice. I'm sure there's an explanation for why he left without leaving a note."

I wriggle out of her grip and shrug. "It is what it is. Just fun. I should have listened to you." Clearing my throat, I step around her and keep walking to the shower. Willow gives me a pitying look as I pass her. I don't want their damn pity.

"Elsie…" I shut the door behind me, not wanting to deal with it. I'm going to swallow my pride and put a smile on my face and roll with whatever comes my way.

After scrubbing away all traces of Aiden, I slip on my clothes and blow-dry my hair. I can't stand soaking wet hair, even if I am going to throw it up in a messy bun right after. When I turn off the dryer, there's silence on the other side of the door. Thank goodness. The girls must have gone. I purposely took my time so I wouldn't have to face them again.

I twist my long brown locks up into a messy bun, straighten my top, and brush my hands down the front of me. I look at the makeup on the countertop and screw my face up then shrug my shoulders. I can't be bothered today.

Stepping into the living area, I pause mid-step while my stomach drops to the floor. "What are you doing here?" I don't bother hiding my bitterness.

The smile that was on Aiden's face drops. "Wh… what do you mean?" He lifts his hand and rubs the back of his neck.

I storm past him to my room. "So, it's normal for you to get what you want and leave?"

"Wait, Elsie. That's not what happened."

I whip around. "How did you even get in here?"

He shoves his hands in the pockets of his jeans. "Addison. She was leaving. She told me to wait, but she didn't warn me about your morning attitude." He chuckles, trying to make light of the situation.

My eyes narrow, and his smile vanishes. "You left and didn't tell me. I didn't think you were like that."

"I'm not. I'm here now. Did you not get my text message?"

Of course, the one place I didn't check. Trust me to overreact for no reason. I left my phone in my bag last night.

I shake my head. After going back to the table, I dig my phone out from under my stuff from yesterday, press the button to light the screen, and there's nothing there, just the time staring back at me.

"Nope, no message."

"What? No. I sent you a message. Here, look on my phone."

I watch as he takes his phone from his back pocket of his jeans. The screen lights up, and his fingers move over the screen. "Oh, man." His hand smacks himself in the forehead. "See? I told you I'm no good with my phone. I wrote the text and mustn't have hit send."

Seconds later, my phone alerts me to a message.

I cock my eyebrow at him. "Are you serious?"

"Just read it, will you?"

I glance down at the screen once again.

> **Aiden:** I had to go to practice. I'll come back and walk with you to your first class.

The anger and annoyance from a second ago slowly leaves my body. I look up at Aiden. His hand runs through his damp hair.

"Sorry," I mutter. "Still, you didn't send it, so my anger is justified."

"Of course. I'd be pissed if you up and left without a note or message." Aiden steps closer; he smells fresh and clean with a hint of aftershave. "Now shut up and give me a kiss." His arms encircle my waist, and mine go around his neck. Our lips connect ever so slightly, like the brush of a feather, and it feels awesome.

I moan. "We should probably stop and go to class, or we won't see the inside of any classrooms today," I breathe against his lips.

Aiden pulls back but still holds onto my waist. "We could skip?" A mischievous grin spreads across his face.

"Nope, sorry. I'm not that girl."

Aiden leans over and pecks my already aching lips. "I know you're not, but it was worth a try."

CHAPTER
Twenty Three

Elsie

We walk across the courtyard, and something is different. A wave of utter happiness rushes from the top of my head right down to my toes, and no matter what happens, I want to be with Aiden.

Glancing around at the people walking by, I turn to him. "So, here's something to think about."

"What's that?" He looks at me as if he wants to devour me right on the spot.

Don't tempt me, buddy.

I clear my throat. I can't believe I'm going to ask this. "What are your thoughts on an actual relationship?"

His forehead pinches together.

I quickly rush more words out before he can speak. "I know you've ended a relationship not that long ago, but I like you. I really like you." *And I could almost love you,* but I leave that off.

"I really like you, too," Aiden says, but he sounds so uncertain.

A sharp pain stabs me in the chest. "Okay, well, I'll leave you with that to do with what you want." I scurry away down the nearest corridor. *Damn, he's so hot and cold.*

I rush off to class, having a schedule full of classes to distract me for most of the day. My phone vibrates in my back pocket. Pulling it out, I purse my lips and sigh at Aiden's name on the screen.

> **Aiden:** I'm sorry if I upset you. That's all I seem to be good at lately. I have to tell you something before anything can be official. Meet me tonight at the basketball court.

I chew my bottom lip, wondering what he could possibly have to tell me. I hit reply.

> **Elsie:** Okay...

It's all I can manage to write for fear of reading something I don't want to see.

Hours later, it's time for lunch, and I head to the café to meet Addison.

"Hey," she greets me. We find a table and drop our butts into the only spare booth. It's one of the busiest times to eat here.

"Hey," I reply, placing my bag by the side of my chair.

Addison leans forward and rests her head on her hands with her elbows on the table. She's giving me a raised eyebrow, what-went-on-last-night kind of look. "So, tell me what happened last night and this morning," she says in a singsong kind of voice.

My cheeks heat up. "Not much to tell…"

She pushes back in her seat. "Oh, don't you hold out on me. Give me details."

I grin stupidly before saying, "Okay." Then, I fill her in on the night with Aiden. Butterflies tickle the inside of my stomach as I recall and think about everything that happened last night.

When I finish, all Addison manages is a breathless, "Wow," and I nod.

"So, what happened this morning with your grumpy attitude?"

"Well, he typed a message to me but didn't hit send. Rookie mistake. All is forgiven. But now he's acting weird, and after I told him I liked him and was implying that I'd like this thing between us to be more, he went funny, and now he has something to tell me."

Before Addison can respond, Parker slides in beside her. "Tell you what?"

I wave my hand. "Don't worry. Just Aiden and his secret—"

"Oh, so he told you that the girlfriend he told you about isn't real. Never was." Parker reaches for a fry on Addison's plate while my stomach plummets to the floor, and my heart cracks.

"What did you say?" Addison turns toward Parker, her eyes becoming slits.

"What? You said he'd told you," Parker replies through a mouthful of fries.

"No, I didn't. You came in on half a conversation. I said he has something to tell me. Is that it? He never really had a g-girlfriend in the first p-place?" My voice cracks, and my chin starts to tremble. Surely, this can't be happening.

I start analyzing the conversations we've had about his girlfriend. He always seemed to go weird when I brought her up. I guess this would explain why. *He lied.*

"Wait a second, how long have you known? Because you came in as if you've known for some time." I point an accusing finger at Parker. He's supposed to be my friend. I turn to Addison, and my eyes narrow. "Did you know? You two share everything, so you must have known." My chest feels as if it might explode, while breathing physically starts to hurt.

Addison's hands go up in defense. "I promise you I didn't know." Her fiery gaze lands on Parker, whose face clearly has paled. "You've known this? For how long?" She pokes a finger into Parker's chest while I watch the exchange.

"The night we went to the movies." Parker's face screws up, and my mouth drops open.

"I can't believe this," I whisper. My head hangs while I try to focus on the half-eaten plate of food in front of me. A million things are running through my head. I want answers. *What am I going to do?*

"Elsie…" Addison's tenderness causes me to look up. She's blurry as tears are filling my eyes and threatening to fall over my lids. "Why would he lie?" I ask breathlessly.

Addison reaches out and takes my hand. "I'm sure there's a good reason for it."

"Perhaps this is why he becomes weird with me when I mention her."

"It would explain a lot." There's bitterness in her words by the tone in her voice.

I turn to look at Parker. "Why didn't you tell me?" It hurts more, knowing Parker knew and didn't bring it to my attention.

"Yes, why didn't you tell us?" Addison chimes in with such anger it sounds like he's going to be in trouble when they get behind closed doors. That's not what I care about right now, though.

"I…" His Adam's apple bobs as he swallows. "I told him that I would give him the chance to tell you first."

"You should have told me." I reach over and pick up my bag, throwing it over my shoulder before storming out of the café.

Addison calls my name, but I don't want to talk right now.

I want answers.

Simple, truthful answers.

And there's only one way to get them.

CHAPTER
Twenty Four

Aiden

Walking out of my last class before lunch, my phone sounds off, alerting me to a message. I finally turned up the volume yesterday in an attempt to try harder. I smile when I see Elsie's name.

Elsie: I need to talk now. Meet me at the court.

Aiden: Everything okay?

Worry fills me as I wait for her reply. Thankfully, I don't have to wait long.

Elsie: No.

With her single-word response, I take off running to find out what's wrong.

Minutes later, I'm pushing through the door into the basketball court, where I laid eyes on Elsie for the second time. When I step inside, I catch her pacing up and down the side of the court.

"Hey, beautiful, what's wrong?" I stride over to her, wanting to wrap her in my arms and assure her that, no matter what, everything will be all right.

When her face meets mine, my feet halt in their tracks. Her face is red and tear-stained.

"Don't you beautiful me, you liar," she grits out from between her teeth while pointing a sharp finger my way.

What's going on?

"What are you talking about?" I move toward her again, but she moves away. She won't let me touch or comfort her.

"You lied," she screams, her face turning beet red.

She knows.

How though?

"You know," I state the obvious.

Elsie's arms fly in the air then move back to her face, where she covers her tears. "Why didn't you tell me from the start? Instead, I found out by the slip of Parker's tongue."

I take in a huge breath. Damn! It was only a matter of time before this came out, and she's right, I should have told her ages ago. "I'm sorry. I did it because I didn't want anyone getting hurt—myself included."

"Bit late for that now. I look like a damn fool." Elsie's legs start moving again, but I need her to stop pacing. I desperately want to hold her, kiss her, and make this all better.

"This was never a fling." My voice rises with each word.

She finally stops pacing and turns my way.

"This between us was—and still is, hopefully—more," I state.

"Pfft… you expect me to believe anything you say now?"

I rush to her, taking her face in my hands. She tries to pull away, but I won't let her. I draw her into my arms and hold her little body against me. "I'm not a liar. I did it to protect myself… and you…" I pause for a moment. She stops trying to escape my grip, so I continue. "I did it to protect myself and anyone else who fell for me. You, especially you. When I first met you in the library, I knew you'd be hard for me to keep away from." My voice softens as I gently hold her out so I can look her in the eyes, for Elsie to see that I'm telling her the truth.

"You could have easily said that you didn't want a relationship. Not that we're even in one." Elsie rolls her eyes. Her eyes are still pink, but thankfully, the tears have stopped. My chest aches at the thought that I brought those tears to the surface. I never, ever intended to hurt Elsie.

"I don't regret us. If anything, the time we've had together has been the best ever. I don't ever want to leave here. If I have to go, then I want you to come with me." I don't miss her breath hitching as I speak, and every single word I've just said is the truth.

Elsie pulls herself out of my arms, crossing hers in front of her.

I've broken her.

My chest aches as I stare at her. The happy Elsie has vanished, and it's all because of me.

"Elsie…" I reach for her while the lump in my throat swells.

"Don't. This…"—she waves her hand between us—"is over. You don't have to worry about anything when you leave. I'm done with this." Elsie doesn't even sound like herself, and I can't believe I've done this to her.

"Please d-don't do t-this." My words crack, just like my heart.

"It's done. Now leave me alone." She picks up her bag and walks out, a shell of the girl I knew this morning.

"Dude, what the hell?" I lash out at Parker.

We're standing in our kitchen, talking, because I couldn't even finish my classes today. My head's all over the place. I can't get the image of broken Elsie out of my mind. Her eyes lost their sparkle, and her brilliant smile faded into my forest of lies.

"Man, I'm so sorry. It just slipped out."

As we are speaking, the door flies open and in charges a raging bull—Addison. Her lips form a thin line, her eyebrows are furrowed, and I can feel the disdain emanating off her.

"How could you do this to her? She trusted you." Addison steps up to me and shoves my shoulder. "Why make up a stupid lie? She would have respected your wishes had you told her from the start that you didn't want anything serious." A frustrated growl rises from her throat. "Why are boys so damn clueless?"

"It wasn't my intention. I know now I've done the wrong thing. How do I fix this, Addison?" I plead.

She takes a seat at the counter. "Don't think you're off the hook either, buddy." She gives Parker a death stare.

"It wasn't my fault. Okay, yes, I helped cover it up, but I was giving him a chance to do it himself." Parker waves his hand toward me from the opposite side of the counter.

"You shouldn't have done that. And as for fixing this, I don't know. She won't talk to me about it." Her voice begins to soften.

"I need to fix this."

"Yes, you do, because the girl I saw before I came here is the lowest I've ever seen her. It breaks my heart that I can't fix this for her. I can yell and carry on at you, but in the end, it's not going to make Elsie feel any better. I suggest you keep trying to reach out to her if it's her you want."

"I want her, and I'm going to fix this."

CHAPTER
Twenty Five

Elsie

I'm numb. The week has been a blur. I even canceled all my tutoring because I can't bring myself to face people. I walked in the door from my classes an hour ago and planted my ass firmly on the couch and have surrounded myself with all the sugary goodness a girl needs in a situation like this.

On the coffee table sits Twinkies, Twizzlers, chocolate ice cream, and plenty of soda. I don't plan to move from this spot all weekend.

Aiden has tried to talk to me through the week, but I've brushed him off. His text messages haven't stopped. Funny how now it seems he's connected himself to his phone again. I get about five messages a day, but I can't bring myself to reply.

My phone vibrates, and I pick it up from the table. It is an email from the mystery man 'A' for tutoring. *What does he want?*

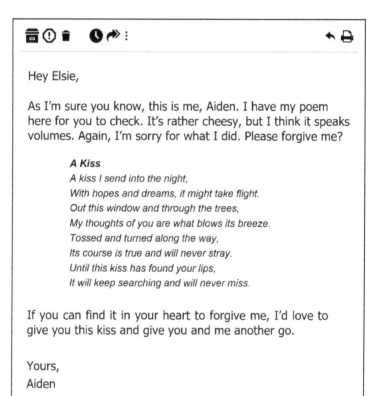

Hey Elsie,

As I'm sure you know, this is me, Aiden. I have my poem here for you to check. It's rather cheesy, but I think it speaks volumes. Again, I'm sorry for what I did. Please forgive me?

> ### A Kiss
> *A kiss I send into the night,*
> *With hopes and dreams, it might take flight.*
> *Out this window and through the trees,*
> *My thoughts of you are what blows its breeze.*
> *Tossed and turned along the way,*
> *Its course is true and will never stray.*
> *Until this kiss has found your lips,*
> *It will keep searching and will never miss.*

If you can find it in your heart to forgive me, I'd love to give you this kiss and give you and me another go.

Yours,
Aiden

Tears drip from my chin as the words from the poem touch my broken heart. The door to the dorm flies open, and the girls walk in just in time to see my fresh lot of tears. I don't know if they're because of my broken heart or if they're because I think he really is sorry.

"Oh, honey." Addison rushes to my side, as do Willow and Jane. All their stares fall on my collection of half-eaten food and wrappers.

"Are you planning to put yourself into a sugar coma this weekend?" Willow laughs.

I shrug. "Doesn't seem like a bad idea to me."

"Nope, you're going to get your ass off that chair and get ready, because we're going out," Addison says.

I'm already shaking my head before she's even finished her sentence. "Nope, not happening. This girl is staying right here." I point to the couch where I'm sitting.

I have three sets of pitying eyes staring at me. Addison stands, looks at me for a moment, then she takes my arm. "Time to stop wallowing. We need to get drunk."

Willow and Jane squeal in excitement. Those two love parties. I used to but not so much anymore.

"I don't want to," I moan, pulling against Addison's tugs.

"I'm not taking no for an answer."

Hours and lots of alcohol later, I'm standing out in front of the boys' house. Music vibrates against the walls, and bodies spill out onto the front lawn.

I don't want to be here.

At least the effects of the tequila are helping me put one foot in front of the other.

Addison hooks her arm through mine and pulls me along with her. I'm wearing a black, fitted dress that sits just above my knee. I didn't want to dress up like I usually would. I'm not out to impress anyone. I'm simply here because they made me. These girls. As much as I love them for trying to take my mind off what's going on, I don't want to take a chance on seeing Aiden.

Maybe he won't be here.

A girl can only dream.

The house is jampacked, as usual, after the huge game they played today. We didn't go like we normally would have. I wonder if Addy is still mad at Parker?

"What's up, girls?" Dane stands in front of us while his eyes scan around, searching.

"She's coming later," I say, knowing full well who he's looking for.

"Ah… yeah, thanks. If you're looking for the rest of the boys, they're out back." We all nod but head in the opposite direction to where the keg sits and is being filled by none other than Clifton.

"Hey there, Elsie." Clifton smiles, leaning over and pulling me into his arms. I fight the urge to pull away, because I know he's drunk. His hands start to move from between my shoulder blades and head south toward my ass.

Thankfully, his hand doesn't make it any further because I'm being reefed away. When I glance around to see who it is, a hard stare passes through me and directly at Clifton. Aiden's hands are clenched by his sides in hard fists. The muscles in his arms tense. "What are you doing touching my girl? Keep your grubby paws off her."

Clifton laughs. A tiny part of me wants to say *I'm not your girl,* but my lips remain shut. "From what I hear, she's not your girl. Never was, actually."

Damn, word spreads fast around here.

Nothing remains a secret.

"Well, what you heard is wrong," Aiden states, his large arms crossing over his tight navy shirt. Damn, he looks good with his hair slicked back and that shirt hugging him in all the right places; it makes me want him even more. Damn, he looks sexy.

"Get over yourself, Aiden. You're gonna leave, and then she'll be all mine."

Aiden releases a puff of air while his face darkens. I grab his arm, not wanting him to get into trouble because of me. He turns toward me.

"Don't." It's all I can manage, and it's enough for Aiden to understand.

"Believe what you want, but she's mine. So, keep your hands to yourself."

"Oh, I'll have fun with her when you're gone." Clifton's laugh is vile and makes my skin crawl in a way I've never experienced before. No guy has ever made me this uncomfortable to be around. I don't even want to be in the same room as Clifton.

It's as though it plays out in slow motion, and yet, I can't stop him. Aiden rushes at Clifton, his hand clenched. Next thing I hear is his fist connecting with Clifton's nose. My hand flies to my mouth, and then it's as if my numb brain switches on.

Aiden stands over Clifton, his breath heaving. I can tell he wants to hit him again, so I reach for his hand, but he flinches away. I reach for Aiden again. His head flicks around, his eyes burn into mine, and I know I need to get Aiden out of this situation and away from Clifton.

"You'll pay for this." Clifton stands, throwing his threat directly at Aiden.

I step in front of Aiden. "Clifton, leave me alone. I'm not interested in dating you. Find a new tutor, because I'm done with you."

Suddenly, I feel a warm hand pressing into mine.

My racing heart calms almost instantly at Aiden's touch.

Clifton scampers away down the hall and out the back. We've drawn the attention of most of the people.

Turning to them, I say, "Carry on, nothing to see here." Then, I spin around to face the guy who still has my hand, and he's taken a firm grip back on my heart.

"Elsie…" Addison runs up to us. Her eyes are focused on me.

"It's okay. I don't think he'll be coming near me again anytime soon," I say.

"Still, I'm sorry."

I release Aiden's hand, and before I know it, I'm pulled into Addison's hug. "It's all good."

Addison releases me and turns to Aiden. "Thanks for helping her when I didn't."

"All good." Aiden stares hungrily at me, and my lower abdomen tingles. "Would you excuse us for a moment? Also, Addison, you need to forgive Parker. He only did what I asked, and he's given me plenty of chances to fix my mistake. Don't blame him for something I've done."

She nods and walks away with the other girls in tow. Aiden takes my hand and hauls me along. I know exactly where we're going when he pulls me into his room and shuts the door behind him. I stand there like the fool that I am while he paces before me.

"I am so sorry, Elsie. Please forgive m-me?" His voice cracks, and my heart tears apart.

"Aiden, I—" My words are swallowed by his mouth as his lips press against mine. Our tongues dance and fight with one another. I know I should be mad at him, but it's as if he's washed away all my anger with a single touch of his lips.

My arms wrap around his neck while his hand moves under my ass and he picks me up. I secure my legs around his waist as he walks me to his queen-sized bed. He places me down and presses his body to mine, grinding against me. His touch is like fire, and I crave it.

"Aiden, stop," I breathe.

He does as I ask and sits up, moving his body to the edge of the bed.

I turn on my side and rest my head in my hand.

"Sorry. I got carried away."

I smile. "That's okay. Look… I want you to know that I forgive you. Doesn't mean you're fully off the hook, because what you did hurt me in so many ways. But I forgive you, and I want this—us—to move forward and put it behind us with a clean slate and no more secrets."

Aiden leans over. "No more secrets," he whispers before placing a featherlight kiss on my lips. "I love you," he breathes against my lips, and the wind rushes from my chest.

My eyes widen as I stare at him.

"I love you, too."

I lean up and kiss him—his lips are my kryptonite.

When we finally come up for air a moment later, he says, "Well, I guess there's just one thing left to do to seal the deal."

My stomach lurches because I know what's coming next.

CHAPTER Twenty Six

Elsie

A week later

"Are we really going to do this?" My legs shake as I stare at the ocean before me. Appearing daunting yet calm, it looks like it's going to swallow me up. I guess the daunting part will eventuate when I actually jump off this rock, fall, and crash into the water below. Addison and Parker have already jumped, and the fear that's taken hold has me cemented in place. Addison screamed as if she was about to be murdered the whole way down, which didn't help me at all.

"Come on, firecracker. You can do this."

Aiden and I teeter on the edge when a gush of wind

makes me unsteady. A scream rips out of my throat. Aiden laughs, and I have an overwhelming urge to push him, but I don't want him to not be prepared and hurt himself.

Aiden reaches out and takes my trembling hand.

"I'm not sure I can do this." I start to take a step back when Aiden tightens his grip, stopping me.

"Do you want to be a failure?" He winks, and my heart stutters in a good way, not the constant heavy beating that's been wreaking havoc on my ribcage over the last few minutes.

"Of course not. This is just so scary." I peek over the edge like I have a hundred times already. Standing here for what feels like an eternity is really unnerving. I need to do this and get it over and done with.

"Consider this a leap of faith into our relationship. You're my girl, Elsie. Jump with me."

Tingles spread from the top of my head and down to my toes. He always knows the right words to say.

I release a heavy breath. "Okay, let's do this."

"That's my girl."

I stare at him and his big, goofy grin that has my girly parts all in a twist. I ready myself on the edge again.

Aiden stands beside me, gripping my trembling hand. "Okay… one, two, three."

It's like something else takes over, and I jump off the rock and scream the entire way down. Seconds later, my body crashes into the water. Swimming back to the surface, my head lifts up and I search for Aiden. He's already swimming over to me.

"How was it?" he asks.

"Exhilarating and refreshing," I breathe. My body's still shaking, and my breath has left me, but it's one experience I won't forget.

I make my way to the shallow water, and as soon as my feet touch the sand, I'm pulled into Aiden's arms. His lips are against mine in seconds.

"I love you," he says between kisses.

"I love you, too."

I mean every word.

I don't know what will happen when it's time for him to leave, but I do know that right now, in this moment, he holds my heart, and I'll probably follow him all over the country if I have to.

I'm his firecracker, and he's my Aussie guy.

Thank you so much for reading My Aussie Guy.
I hope you love Elsie and Aiden as much as I do.

Turn the page to read the first chapter of
My Forbidden Guy (My Guy Series Book 3)

Grab your copy from books2read.com/u/49lAYJ

keep up to date with what's happening, sign up for my Newsletter
app.mailerlite.com/webforms/landing/w4c9g7

Or join my readers group **Lovelock's Flock**
facebook.com/groups/742675105787263

My Forbidden Guy (My Guy Series Book 3)

Chapter One
Paislee

"Hey, what are you thinking about?"

Lifting my head off Dane's chest, I stare into his beautiful chocolate-swirl eyes and run my fingers through his now longish hair. *This man takes my breath away.*

Dane's hand meets my cheek briefly then brushes some stray sandy-blonde strands away from my face.

"I was thinking about when we first met." I smile. His touch causes my heart to skip a beat.

Dane chuckles. "You acted like this stuttering little schoolgirl."

I recall the memory when he came to our house for the first time and Parker introduced us. I was such an embarrassment.

I smack his bare chest while laughing. "Shut up!"

Dane becomes silent as his eyes bore into mine. "You captured my heart the moment Parker introduced us. All I can say is that I'm glad you didn't give up on us, even if it meant keeping things from Parker." Tightness pulls at my chest, and it's not a good one.

Parker still doesn't know, and we've both agreed it's best if we don't tell him. And now, here I am, lying in Dane's bed, with my brother down the hall.

I open my mouth to respond when voices echo outside Dane's door. Our heads whip around when the voices become louder.

"He should be up by now," Parker yells down the hallway.

Before I can manage to scramble up and out of bed, Dane sits up. His hands push my side, and he shoves me off the bed like one would do to dirty clothes. The wind leaves my lungs as I hit the carpeted floor hard. I go to stand and give him a piece of my mind when his door flies open, so I press my body as close to the bed as I can in an attempt to hide.

Thankfully, whoever is at the door will not be able to see me from where they're currently standing. I'm wedged between the wall and the bed. I can't say I've ever been tossed from the bed like I was nothing before.

To be honest, it doesn't sit right with me.

We should come clean about our relationship to Parker.

It's the right thing to do—for Parker and for us.

It's past time.

These last couple of months and all this sneaking around have been fun, but I think we're heading into the more serious part of our friendship. *Or is it a relationship?* I have no idea. You'd think we're officially a couple, only we're not. For some reason, we have been avoiding that conversation like the plague.

Now, here I am, hiding from my brother who's standing in the doorway.

"Get up! We've got classes in thirty minutes."

"Yeah, who could miss you yelling down the hall," Dane bites back as if he's just been woken up.

I don't dare breathe.

Please don't walk into the room, I beg.

"Shut up and get up." I hear Parker's laughter.

These guys love to stir each other up.

Sometimes, I think Parker wishes he had gotten a brother instead of me.

The door finally slams shut, and I bounce off the floor like I am spring-loaded.

"Sorry," Dane whispers as he rushes off the bed and goes to take me into his arms.

Holding out my hands, I stop him. "Don't. Perhaps this…"—I wave my hand between us—"whatever it is, has run its course. I'm not the kind of girl who deserves to be kicked off the bed and forced to hide on the floor," I grind out through clenched teeth.

Anger.

That word doesn't even begin to describe the feelings pulsating through my veins.

Hurt.

There's so much hurt.

Shame.

I am totally embarrassed.

I blink furiously, pushing away the wetness that wants to cloud my vision.

"No, Pais. Please, don't do this. I'm so sorry. I panicked." Dane tries again to pull me into his arms, but I shove him hard in the chest then pick up my shirt and shorts from the floor. They were also pushed to the side by Dane so they wouldn't be seen by my brother. Everyone else knows about us, although I'm not sure about Jimmy, Willow, or Jane. I don't know them well enough to include them in my private business.

Pulling my top over my head, I turn to Dane. His eyes widen.

"Look, yes, I'm angry. Maybe you need to think about what it is you really want, and if I'm one of those things, then perhaps we need to make this official… and tell Parker." His eyes meet mine, but now they're bordering on rising panic. "I'll give you some time to think about it."

Dane doesn't reply; he simply lets me walk out the door where I dart across to the bathroom opposite Dane's room. This is my usual escape route.

"Pais?"

I pause mid-step. Turning, my eyes raise to meet Addison's, and I heave a sigh of relief. At least it's her, because she knows our secret.

"What are you doing here?" Addison's voice is low. "Parker's here."

Before I can open my mouth, I hear Parker's voice from behind me. "Hey, Paislee, what are you doing here?"

My heart hammers against my chest.

"Oh, I'm just—"

Addison cuts me off with, "She's meeting me. I asked her over so we can grab a bite to eat." Addison smiles sweetly at Parker, who simply shrugs and walks past us.

"Okay, have fun. I'll see you after classes."

"See ya," Addison and I say in unison.

When Parker's out of earshot, Addison's heavy stare turns on me.

Dane's door flies open. "Catch you later," he says when he drops his gaze and slips around us.

Great, now I've made things super awkward.

"Perfect," I mutter.

Moments ago, everything was great.

Now? I don't even know where I stand with Dane.

Want more?
Get your copy of My Forbidden Guy now!
books2read.com/u/49lAYJ

To keep up to date with what's happening, sign up for my Newsletter
at app.mailerlite.com/webforms/landing/w4c9g7

Lost Series
The Lost One—Book One
The Missing One—Book Two
Lost Series Boxed Set

Letters in Blood Series
Dear Captor—Book One
With Love—Book Two
Forever Yours—Book Three
Dear Captor Boxed Set

My Guy Series
Monday Night Guy – Book One
My Aussie Guy – Book Two
My Forbidden Guy – Book Three
The Right Guy – Book Four
My Guy Series Complete Boxed Set

ALSO BY
Liz Lovelock

The Jilted Series
Something Old – Book One
Something New – Book Two
Something Borrowed – Book Three
Something Blue – Book Four
Something Beautiful – Book Five – A Novella

ABOUT THE Author

I'm a wife, mother, reader, blogger, and now an author. I'm always busy doing something as I have so much going on, and my three little ones keep me on my toes.

I'm from bright and sunny Queensland, Australia. I have always been a reader. When I was little, I would be up late reading *Garfield* and *Asterix* comic books and also *Footrot Flats*. When I hit high school, they gave us *Tomorrow When the War Began* by John Marsden, and from there my love of books continued to grow.

I keep a notebook and pen beside my bed for when those late-night ideas pop into my head, plus I'm a stationery addict and love pens, notebooks, and, well, anything stationery.

ACKNOWLEDGEMENTS

I'll say sorry first in case I miss anyone.

I'd like to thank my editors—Lauren Clarke from Lauren Clarke Editing and Kaylene Osborn from Swish Design & Editing. And to my proofreader, Jenn from Jenn Lockwood Editing. Without you ladies, I'd be thoroughly lost. You've both pushed me with this one. Thank you for fitting me in on short notice and polishing up my work to make it squeaky clean. You're awesome! Thanks for all your advice and guidance.

To my fantastic team of betas—Halle, Abbey, and Melissa. Your input is so valuable. Thank you for all your feedback—you're all amazing. And thanks for being patient and pushing me to do better.

A huge thank you to Ben from Be Designs for designing the perfect cover and working with me until I was happy. It is everything I wanted it to be. I love it!

Thanks, Reggie Deanching, for a beautiful photograph of Cody Smith and Tionna Petramalo. You're all amazing.

These next mentions are my other halves in the author world. Without their constant support and friendship, I may have given up a long time ago. They're my cyber sisters spread far and wide around Australia and America, so thank you to Jemma Brown aka JB Heller, KE Osborn, Kaylene Osborn, and Belle Brooks. These ladies are truly amazing. I'd be lost without our chats.

To Anastasia—your help has been incredible. Without you and your input, I'd be all over the place.

To my Flock—I love you, girls. Your support is truly nothing short of amazing. I know I have a safe place in my group with you all. Thank you.

To my readers—I feel blessed to have your continuous support. Thank you.

To my family and my husband—you're truly wonderful. You've never given up on me. You sit and listen when I need to vent out my frustrations, never once complaining about it. I love you.

To my three beautiful children—Millie, Cale, and Finn. You three test my patience, but I'm so grateful to have you in my life to love. Families are forever.

CONNECT WITH
Liz online

TikTok
tiktok.com/@lizlovelockauthor

Twitter
twitter.com/LizLovelock

Email
lizlovelockauthor@gmail.com

Website
lizlovelockauthor.com

Facebook
facebook.com/people/Liz-Lovelock-
Author/100008389321975/

Goodreads
goodreads.com/author/show/8268717.Liz_Lovelock

Instagram
instagram.com/lizlovelock/

Or sign up for my **Newsletter**
app.mailerlite.com/webforms/landing/w4c9g7

Lightning Source UK Ltd.
Milton Keynes UK
UKHW010707270223
417728UK00001B/278